the True Colour *of the* Sea

Robert Drewe is the author of seven novels, four books of short stories, two memoirs and two plays. His work has been widely translated, and adapted for film, television, theatre and radio.

ALSO BY ROBERT DREWE

Novels
The Savage Crows
A Cry in the Jungle Bar
Fortune
Our Sunshine
The Drowner
Grace
Whipbird

Short stories
The Bodysurfers
The Bay of Contented Men
The Rip

Memoir
The Shark Net
Montebello

Plays
The Bodysurfers: The Play
South American Barbecue

Sketches
Walking Ella
The Local Wildlife
Swimming to the Moon
The Beach: An Australian Passion

Co-productions
Sand (with John Kinsella)
Perth (with Frances Andrijich)

As editor
The Penguin Book of the Beach
The Penguin Book of the City
The Best Australian Short Stories 2006
The Best Australian Short Stories 2007
The Best Australian Essays 2010

the True Colour *of the* Sea

ROBERT DREWE

HAMISH HAMILTON
an imprint of
PENGUIN BOOKS

HAMISH HAMILTON

UK | USA | Canada | Ireland | Australia
India | New Zealand | South Africa | China

Penguin Books is part of the Penguin Random House group of companies
whose addresses can be found at global.penguinrandomhouse.com.

First published by Penguin Random House Australia Pty Ltd, 2018

1 3 5 7 9 10 8 6 4 2

Cover design by Alex Ross © Penguin Random House Australia Pty Ltd
Cover artwork from detail of 'With the Tide' linocut by Mariann Johansen-Ellis,
www.mariannjohansen-ellis.com
Text design by Midland Typesetters
Typeset in Adobe Caslon Pro 11.75/16.5 by Midland Typesetters, Australia
Printed and bound in Australia by Griffin Press, an accredited ISO AS/NZS 14001
Environmental Management Systems printer

A catalogue record for this
book is available from the
National Library of Australia

ISBN: 978 0 14378 268 1

penguin.com.au

For Tray

'To undiscovered waters, undreamed shores.'

William Shakespeare

'Time is short and the water is rising.'

Raymond Carver

Contents

Dr Pacific

Don dropped dead on the sand and that was that. We'd just finished our lighthouse walk and he bent down to remove his shoes for our swim and keeled over. He was in his blue board shorts with the red palm trees. One shoe on and one shoe off when the ambulance took him – his new Rockport walkers. Only seventy-eight. Three years ago now and as I said, that was that.

Since that moment the days often look blurry around the edges, like I'm wearing his glasses by mistake. People loom around corners when I don't expect them and next minute they're on the doorstep. Jehovahs. Seventh-dayers. Charity collectors.

A Green type of woman in drifty clothes came by wanting to save baby fruit bats. She said the cold snap was making them lose their grip and fall out of the trees and they needed to be wrapped up in bandanas and fed mango smoothies. She was collecting money to provide the bandanas and smoothies and she showed me a photo of a baby bat in a red bandana to clinch the deal.

'Look how cute it is, peeping out snug and warm,' she said.

'Cuteness is a survival characteristic of baby animals,' I said. 'If you ask me, this one looks a bit confused being right side up instead of hanging upside down.'

'But very cute, you must admit,' she said, shaking her Save the Grey-Headed Flying Fox collection tin. It hardly rattled. She was one of those North Coast women who look better from a distance.

The reason I was unsympathetic was that we've got hundreds of flying foxes living in a colony in our street, raiding our fruit trees and screeching all night and doing their business all over our decks, especially the Hassetts' and the Rasmussens', and the council playground so kids can't play outdoors, and probably spreading the Hendra virus or Ebola or something.

Even worse than their noise and mess and being kept awake all night, the most irritating thing about them is they take only one bite out of each piece of fruit. They like to sample one bite out of every papaya and mango and mandarin on the coast – and they ruin the lot. And of course they're protected under the Wildlife Act.

Mind you, there's even people around here who are fond of brown snakes, the ones that kill you quickest. Those people need a slap, honestly. And down at Broken Head there used to be signs saying *Do Not Molest the Sharks.* The tourists pinched all the signs for souvenirs.

I said to her, 'Let nature take its course, miss. If I was a fruit bat and the weather got too nippy, I wouldn't wait for a bandanna. I'd up stakes and fly to North Queensland.'

Another day a young woman with a bossy accent called in to convince the 'household' to switch to a different electricity provider. Sun-Co or North-Sun or something. There were lots of benefits for the 'household' in switching to Sun-Co, she said.

I told her it wasn't much of a household any more. 'Just this gnarly old bird.'

'You should go solar and save yourself many dollars,' she insisted, in a South African sort of voice. 'The sun is so harsh here you might as well benefit financially from it.'

The way she said 'harsh' it sounded like 'horsh'. Then she looked me up and down in a superior way. 'Your skin looks like you enjoy plenty of sun.'

I let that go. 'I certainly do,' I said, and gave her a big sunny grin. 'I swim every day, rain or shine. I've earned every one of these wrinkles.'

At eighty you can choose which insults you respond to. I said the stove was gas and I just used electricity to run the TV and boil the kettle. I told her I only ate cheese sandwiches and the pensioners' ten-dollar three-course special at the bowling club. A glass of brown rum of an evening. No point cooking for one.

I said, 'Miss, when it's dark and cold I just creep into bed like the decrepit old widow I am.'

She raised her drawn-on eyebrows and cut short her electricity spiel then, like I was one of those eccentric old witches with bird's nest hair and forty-three cats. Maybe I'd laid the elderly stuff on too thick. But she was a hard-faced girl.

*

Ever notice that after people pass away the world seems to have more sunsets than dawns? I try to avoid sunsets. They stand for things being over. With sunsets I think of Don in his palm-tree board shorts swimming over the trees and hills into those pink and gold clouds – that exaggerated heaven you see in the pamphlets the Jehovahs' hand out. And our darling boy Nathan and his friend Carlos in '87. My own mum and dad. Oh, sunsets draw the sadness out.

When that sunset feeling seeps in, watch out. Don't think about everyone gone, and no grandchildren. Sorrow shows in your face. Stay upbeat and busy is my motto. Don't worry yourself about last words, either. (Don's final word he bubbled out on the sand sounded like 'Thursday' or 'birthday' – I've stopped wondering what it meant.) And I don't blame Carlos any more for making Nathan sick. I try to face east and the dawn and the beginning of things.

Just after sun-up every morning, all seasons, I do my lighthouse walk. It's always interesting – big blue jellyfish the size of bin lids lying there; sometimes an octopus or little stingray beached in a rock pool. One morning the shore was strewn with hundreds of green capsicums, as if a capsicum freighter had jettisoned them. All green, no red ones, just floating there like blow-up bath toys.

What I enjoy these days is stopping to pick up shells and stones and interesting bits of driftwood to take home. I look for those rare stones shaped like hearts.

Don called this stuff 'flotsam'. He hated beach decor. 'Listen, Bet. Are we doing our exercise or picking up flotsam?' he'd say.

'Who wants to live in a beachcomber's shack?' He preferred the surfaces kept clear for his barometer collection and shiny brass telescope and sudoku books and his memoirs of cricketers and politicians. Books with deadly-dull titles. *Afternoon Light* and *Cabinet Diary* and *A Good Innings*. God save us!

After my walk I leave the morning's beach souvenirs on my towel and then I'm in the sea, swimming the kilometre from The Pass to Main Beach like Don and I used to.

One thing's for sure – it's my love of the ocean that keeps me going. You know what I call the ocean? *Dr Pacific.* All I need to keep me fit and healthy is my daily consultation with Dr Pacific.

'Morning!' I yell out to the surfers waxing their boards on the sand, zipping up their steamers. 'I'm off to see the Doctor!'

Some of the boys give me a friendly wave. They treat me like I'm their crazy brown granny. 'Morning, Bet! Looking good!' They can't wait to hit the surf and ride those barrels. 'They're pumping today!' they yell.

You see things out there – fish galore, and there's a pod of dolphins that lives off the Cape, plus many turtles. And shapes and shadows. Sometimes there's a splash nearby, but I just keep going. I imagine the shadow and splash is Don still swimming alongside me.

*

We're on the trailing edge of tropical cyclones here on the country's most easterly point. One moment it's a hot summer's day and then Cyclone Norman or Cyclone Sharon spins south with its high winds, choppy surf and water spouts, little tornadoes twirling across the ocean. The humidity drives us locals out onto our decks. Everyone sits there with their beers and hibachis and watches the weather over the sea like it's the Discovery Channel.

It's all to do with La Niña or El Niño or something. Firstly, clouds bank up over the fishing boats and container ships on the horizon, then the sky turns thundery and purple, the sea looks sulky and there's distant sheet lightning over the Gold Coast. You can smell the storm racing south. The air smells of meat.

The wind's blowing barbecue smoke into your face. Pressure builds up in your ears. Then a yellowish mist drops over the ocean and hailstones begin pelting down. By now the fruit bats have got night and day mixed up and they start shrieking in this strange muddy daylight as if the sky's falling.

Just as quickly the hail stops, like a tap's been turned off, the sky's clear and the wind moves offshore. The waves spray backwards against the tide in lines of spindrift. The air's so sharp you can see the humpbacks breaching on their way back to the Antarctic.

Funny how the cyclone weather gets all the bachelor whales over-stimulated. The sea's getting strangely warm for them here and they start displaying for the girl whales. Slapping their tails on the water, showing off like teenage boys. Slap, slap, over and over.

*

During Cyclone Sharon we were all out on our decks every day for a week. Even the main bat victims, the Rasmussens and Hassetts. Curiosity and anxiety plus a faint shred of hope brought everyone out. It was bedlam with the noise of the coastguard helicopters and the spotter planes and the lifesavers in their rubber duckies and jetskis and the water-police launches. Up and down the shoreline and river mouths they were searching for poor Gavin Monaghetti.

What happened was Gavin's prawn trawler, the *Tropic Lass,* overturned at night in the cyclone seas off Cape Byron. Gavin and his two young deckhands were believed lost. But next afternoon, the youngest boy, Lachie Pascall, crawled up on Belongil Beach.

Lachie had been guided by the lighthouse and swum fourteen kilometres to shore. He was exhausted, flat as a tack, but he told the rescue services approximately where the boat had sunk.

He said he'd left the others clinging to floating stuff when he set off to swim to land. So they concentrated the hunt and, you wouldn't believe it, six hours later they found Brendan Hess, the second boy. Brendan was just alive. He was badly sun-blistered and dehydrated and hugging an icebox. They had to prise his fingers off it.

For a day or so that gave everyone hope. Brendan said the last he'd seen of Gavin he was clutching a marker buoy. But now there was no sign of him, and after another five days the search for him was called off.

Very sad. I knew poor Gavin. His boat operated out of the Brunswick Heads fishermen's marina and when he wasn't at sea he was a regular drinker down at the bowling club on Friday and Saturday nights. He was quite a big wheel – on the club committee and everything.

'How's my surfer chick?' he'd call out. He liked to flirt with me in a teasing way. 'Still fighting the surfers off, Betty?' he'd say. 'If only I stood a chance!'

'Too young for me,' I'd shoot back. 'I'm no cougar.' Gavin was late sixties, I'm guessing. A good-looking silvery fellow. Lovely smile. The dashing, cheeky sort I used to go for before Don came along. Solid, responsible Don. Good business brain. 'You can't go wrong there,' my old dad said, more than once. I guess I didn't.

Gavin knew I liked a rum or two of an evening. During the bingo he'd sneak a mojito onto the table for me when I wasn't looking. Once he pinched a hibiscus flower off the bush by the club's entrance and left it alongside the drink.

*

That strange time of Cyclone Sharon I'd be walking home from my meal at the bowling club about nine – it's only a couple of blocks – and I'd look up and the sky would be thronging with dopey fruit bats caught in the lighthouse beam. Flapping wilder than usual, squealing, and crashing into trees and electricity wires. Bats were even on the sand and struggling in the shallows. Where's your famous radar now? I wondered.

The colony had started raiding the local coffee plantations. They'd chewed up thousands of dollars' worth of ripe beans and the local growers were in a panic. As usual, Parks and Wildlife was no help.

'The grey-headed flying fox is a protected coastal species,' they said. Blah, blah. 'Try scare guns or netting the plantations.' But the nets were too expensive and the fake guns only made the bats shriek and act crazier, especially now they were addicted to coffee.

As their caffeine habit increased, the bats became even more speedy and twitchy. Their flying was more reckless, their screeching and squabbles were even shriller than usual. And they began to fall off the perch.

It took a while but the survivors eventually woke up to themselves and threw off their caffeine addiction. Mind you, there wasn't much left to eat around here by then. One full moon there was a great squawking and flapping, as if they'd come to a decision, and what was left of the colony upped stakes and flew north into the wind.

Carol Hassett's house had taken the brunt of their droppings and noise. Carol said she hoped they all had headaches from coffee withdrawal.

*

I was on my morning lighthouse walk at low tide. It was three or four weeks after the latest cyclone had rearranged the shoreline and something not regular, a bump on the smoothness, caught my eye on the hard-packed sand. A big shiny white bone had just washed up.

I stopped and picked it up. It hadn't been long in the sea. No weed was growing on it, and it wasn't eroded. It didn't look like any animal bone I could recall. Thick, quite heavy, it was about as long as – I'm sorry to say – a human thighbone.

I know I think about things too much these days. If I'm not careful my imagination runs away with me. But as I turned it over in my hand, boy, I had that prickly sensation on the back of my neck. This old duck almost passed out there on the shore.

I said to myself, 'Betty, you're holding a thighbone in your hand!' The sides were smooth and one end of the bone was cleanly snapped. At its widest end the bone was jagged, with a zigzag edge of sharp points, as if it had been severed by a big pair of pinking shears.

I held the white bone with the zigzag edge and my neck did that prickly thing. I was thinking of the search for Gavin, and of his friendly ways, and his silvery looks, and of what I now presumed had happened to him. It took all my concentration not to collapse on the sand.

What should I do with the bone? Take it to the Byron Bay police? The cops would probably laugh it off as bait from a lobster pot or garbage thrown from a ship. ('This lady thinks she's found a femur, sergeant!')

Lots of thoughts struck me. If it was Gavin's thighbone, would his next of kin appreciate its discovery? (He was close to his three daughters and he had an ex-wife somewhere.) Wouldn't the evidence of the bone – that sharp, zigzag pattern – be too brutal for his girls? Shouldn't there be a *thingamajig*, a DNA test? Could you hold a funeral service for a femur?

Anyway, what amount of remains, what percentage of flesh or bone was necessary for a trace of a person to be counted as a body? Would a leg bone count? Did it have a soul? I'm not a religious woman – I don't know these things. What would my pesky Jehovahs and Seventh-dayers say? God's in nature is all I believe.

Oh, I worried over all this. The white bone in my hand now had huge significance. It carried the weight of many emotions. In the bright beach glare it had what the local hippie chicks would call an *aura*. A pale but powerful aura. The aura of a handsome kind man who'd suffered a violent death.

I continued my walk while I thought about what to do. And I decided I wanted to keep the white thighbone. I wanted to treasure the memory of poor Gavin Monaghetti. I wanted to be able to look at the femur and recall his smile and the gift mojitos and the hibiscus on the bingo table.

I had no pockets and the bone was too cumbersome to carry, so I placed it on a patch of dry sand securely far from the water, and jammed a driftwood branch into the ground to mark the spot. I'd pick it up on my way back.

Of course, as I trudged along I started feeling guilty about Don. I had no treasured souvenirs of poor Don (I'd given his cricketers' and politicians' memoirs to the Rotary market stall). All I had were his clothes hanging in his side of the wardrobe, getting musty and moth-holed, but with his smell still faintly on them. Jackets and sweaters I was too sentimental to give to the op shop. His Rockport walkers growing mould. The palm-tree board-shorts the hospital gave back to me.

How would Don feel about me having another man's thighbone on the mantelpiece? Because already that's where I was imagining putting Gavin's femur – over the fireplace, mounted on a little stand like the gold brackets that held Don's brass telescope. (Yes, on that very same telescope-stand.) With its pale aura gleaming out into the room, through the windows and out to sea.

I felt strangely unfaithful and wicked for most of the walk, but young and reckless as well, almost like a teenager. My brain was fizzing with excitement. Sorry, Don.

I picked up the pace on my way back. I was hurrying along the shore to grab up the bone to take home. I reached the spot I'd marked with the driftwood branch but the marker was gone. The tide was still fairly low but obviously a contrary set of waves had swept over the patch of sand, scooped it clean of debris, left it smooth and bare as a tabletop, swamped it so recently that air bubbles were still popping on its surface.

That's not unusual, of course. Waves and tides and winds seem irregular forces of nature, erratic in their evenness, but there's always a proper reason for their existence, like Cyclone Sharon being caused by rapidly warming seas.

I understand all that. I'm an old North Coast girl. I see this every day. More than anyone, I understand the way Dr Pacific does things. So I waded into the sea, into that shallow green dip between the shore break and the shore itself, and the bone was lying on the seabed, rolling back and forth in the tide. Quite easy to find, being so pale.

Another Word for Cannibals

In the late afternoon the descendants of the cannibals' victim lined up warily side-by-side outside the church in the island's village square. Flowers and balloons decorated the square and three old women stood and moaned to music on the back of a truck. The balloons tossed and twisted in gusts from the ocean and palms lashed back and forth. Facing each of the descendants, staring deeply into their eyes, stood a descendant of someone who'd eaten their ancestor.

Now a helicopter rose above the headland and clattered over the square, showering the crowd with sand and setting the village dogs cringing and barking, before disappearing into the hinterland. A loudspeaker crackled, the music and keening stopped and a deep male voice made an announcement in Pijin that the visitors didn't understand. In the silence that followed they became aware of the surf breaking against the outer reef, the wind rattling the palms and the low sunrays filtering across the square.

To identify their unique status, the victim's successors and their partners had been given special island clothes to wear: outsized red and green flowered shirts and dresses, all of the same material, made by the village women, obviously to local measurements for they hung loosely on the visitors and flapped in the breeze. The cannibals' male heirs, meanwhile, wore only woven palm loincloths and their heads and their bodies were painted to resemble skeletons.

Drumming started up suddenly in the background and the skeleton-men began panting in unison and stamping their feet to the beat. The skull-mouth of the cannibal descendant in front of Damian Horne was red from chewing betel nut and the man loomed so close that Damian felt the pungent heat of his breath on his face.

Averting his head from the man's heavy exhalations, Damian attempted a calming smile and sympathetic wink at Lisa, his flustered wife, who was simultaneously trying to subdue her billowing dress while avoiding the panting breath of an even larger skeleton-man.

Damian's wink was intended to remind Lisa of their honoured status here on this remote atoll in the central Pacific where the cultures of Polynesia, Melanesia and Micronesia lapped over the coral reefs and flowed into each other. It was meant to convey things like *Relax, Leez. I know this seems crazy, but let's appreciate the uniqueness of our bizarre situation, a once-in-a-lifetime experience. We're their guests. Just go with it.*

Flecks of red juice flew from the chin of Damian's islander attendant. Over the drumming, the old women started keening again. Damian's wink hadn't calmed Lisa. An indoor-looking woman, his wife appeared too frail and urban against this tropical-island decor. From the moment the *Reef Explorer* had sailed away and left them there, she'd turned pale. Her whole aspect clashed and he hoped she wasn't about to faint.

*

In Sydney, Damian worked in IT and Lisa edited *Bibelot,* a smart interior-design magazine. Their journey to the island of Okina, where Damian's great-great-great-grandfather, the Reverend Isaac Horne, an English Methodist missionary, had been killed and eaten in 1867, had begun eighteen months before with a flurry of emails from a distant cousin, Dr Jennifer Horne-Smith in Leeds. These were followed by a string of back-and-forth correspondence with other Isaac Horne descendants, including Bradley Horne in San Francisco, Kevin Horne in Auckland, Catherine Underhill in Melbourne and Julie Truscott in Adelaide.

'The islanders of Okina want to hold a special 150th-anniversary ceremony to make amends to the Horne descendants,' declared Dr Horne-Smith's initial message. 'I've been asked for the family's reaction. A sensitive matter, as you can imagine. What do you think? I must say I strongly support it myself.'

Her academic interest in traditional Pacific Island carvings, weapons and domestic implements had led to Jennifer, an associate professor at the Institute of Social and Cultural Anthropology at the University of Leeds, meeting George Bogenvanu, Okina's representative in the Pacific Islands Forum, when he accompanied a collection of Okinan artefacts to the Pacifica Exhibition at the British Museum eighteen months before.

Over drinks at the exhibition's opening party, an animated Jennifer soon let George Bogenvanu know that her cultural appreciation of the island of Okina extended beyond battle clubs, kava bowls and penis gourds. After two wines it was somehow thrilling to approach him and announce, a little hectically, 'Your ancestor ate my ancestor.'

She'd thought he might frown or grin uncomfortably but George Bogenvanu, a suave man in his mid-fifties, with the height and bulk of a former international rugby front-rower for Fiji, replied, 'Yes, you're right. I want to talk to you about it.'

Over dinner and more drinks afterwards they discussed Okina in some depth. And especially their rarest of ancestral links: the manner and immediate aftermath of Isaac Horne's death.

As she solemnly told George Bogenvanu, 'The events of that day on Okina are the reason I do what I do.'

'I understand,' he said, his manner as grave as hers, and presently she found herself studying his mouth, considering the square white teeth, how similar each big tooth was to the one next to it, and the vigorous movement of his jaws as he bit into his beef Wellington. A muscle twitched below his ear as he chewed. When he downed his shiraz, his neck swelled as he swallowed.

'How long are you in England?' she asked. Another week, as it turned out. She imagined his teeth biting into her living flesh. 'Let me show you around,' she said.

The correspondence that ensued from Jennifer to the various Horne cousins had stressed the sacred nature of the practice of cannibalism.

'What a pity there isn't another word for it,' she wrote. 'One with less emotional freight. Yes, we could say "anthropophagy", and cannibals could be termed "anthropophagites" or even "anthropophaginians". But these unwieldy terms (such "mouthfuls", more flippant people might joke!) don't stand a chance against the word in common usage, that much-relished name for people who ate people: *Cannibals!*'

As her emails emphasised, 'Contrary to cannibals in popular fiction and the occasional modern man-eating psychopath, Pacific Island cannibals didn't think *Missionaries are delicious. Let's have this one for dinner*. It was part of their traditional culture, to absorb the power of an enemy.'

Clearly, she went on, their ancestor Isaac, who'd voyaged around the Pacific in the mid-nineteenth century establishing Methodism outposts and training local converts, was eaten because as a Christian churchman he represented to the Okinans the threat of European civilisation.

Damian and Lisa had met Jennifer only once before, at a family wedding in north London, and remembered her as a wiry extrovert with reckless scarlet hair and a sort of ethnic-Victorian dress style, a mixture of tinkling bracelets and fingerless net gloves. Today, on the island of Okina, dwarfed by another huge islander and, like Lisa, swimming inside a capacious muu-muu, her self-assurance looked only slightly dented. The way she was gazing gaily about her, and humming to the beat of all the drumming and panting, gave the impression she was perfectly in tune with the proceedings.

Her sandalled feet and ankle bracelets now joined the ritual stamping, and as her fixed smile and jangling jewellery declared

This is all part of the Big Picture, Damian recalled her emailed responses to the descendants' curiosity and their understandably ignorant questions.

'In any society or culture, in whatever period of history, everything we humans do rests on the assumptions we share with our family, friends, neighbours and workmates,' she'd replied.

'Everything social is open to question, including solidly held beliefs and ideas about karma, the self in society, and nature and culture. Only by relating uncritically to the different versions of the world can we be fully human.'

'I'm not clear on this,' Lisa had wondered. 'Is she lecturing us that cannibalism is okay in some circumstances? That if we're against killing people and eating them we aren't fully human?'

'Grandpa Isaac might beg to differ,' Damian had said. 'Frankly, I thought this was one case when we weren't the bad guys.'

In her emails Jennifer had gone on to mention the valuable work her department did to enlighten the First World on the human condition – cannibals and all. 'Through our interest in "exotic" places, social and cultural anthropology considers people, all of us, as social beings.'

She went on, more specifically, 'Reconciliation is very important to the Okinan ethos. But "making amends" isn't the whole point. "Saying sorry" is part of it, but reconciliation ceremonies require something from each side.'

George Bogenvanu had stressed this to her in London. 'There has to be an element of exchange,' he'd said several times.

Exchange? 'So they entertain us in a big way, say sorry for eating him, and then want something from us in return? Some sort of swap?' Damian said. 'Maybe we should remind them that our team is already one member down.'

Not worth getting upset about, though. Isaac's fate was macabre and tragic, but it had made for an extraordinary family legend, not to mention unbeatable dinner-party conversation. Black humour in spades. Of course cannibal jokes were bad form these days. Cannibals were the stuff of old cartoons and comic strips. Chubby cannibals wearing chefs' hats and bones in their noses. Pith-helmeted explorers simmering in big cooking pots.

Everyone drew a polite veil over bloodthirsty bygone practices. Keep shtum about headhunters. Don't mention Michael Rockefeller's mysterious disappearance. But it was the Okinans themselves who'd brought up their old fierce habit and suggested the reconciliation ceremony. Maybe he and Lisa could combine the event with a Pacific Islands vacation.

He'd looked up everything Okinan online. Interesting stuff: like the inbreeding and recessive gene that meant twenty per cent of the population was completely colourblind and only saw things dimly in black and white. And the island custom of burying their dead very deep because of the orange land crabs.

'I'm also thinking style ideas for *Bibelot*,' he told Lisa. 'Atoll-inspired designs. I'm seeing summery basics incorporating jungle ridges of black volcanic rock entwined with snowy coral sands and swathed in emerald rainforest.'

She rolled her eyes. He liked to tease her with this gibberish. A worn-out joke after twelve years.

'I'm seeing whimsical sea-change prints of happy islanders chowing down on clergymen's thighs.'

'Don't mock.' But as nothing more was heard from Jennifer, the reconciliation suggestion gradually slipped away, only recalled when an article on cannibalism leapt out at Damian from *The Guardian* several months later.

Not an everyday news topic. *How many calories would you get from consuming a human body?* So pondered Dr Malcolm Woolhouse, an archaeologist at the University of Sydney. About 118,000 calories, he'd estimated.

With the cooperation of the science and medicine faculties and the university's Institute of Nutrition and Dianetics (and five average-sized adult male cadavers), his 'morbid curiosity', as Dr Woolhouse put it, had led him to publish, in the archaeological journal *Remains,* a calorie-counting guide for cannibals.

In the guide, reprinted in *The Guardian,* Dr Woolhouse, whose speciality was the behaviour of ancient humans, said these hominids might have practised cannibalism for many cultural motives. Or was it for nutritional reasons?

'So how nutritious are we?' he wondered.

To test whether early humans ate people for survival, Dr Woolhouse had investigated whether compared to other mammals they hunted, such as deer, bears and mammoths, human meat offered a nourishing meal.

While admitting his five-man sample was small (and provided no insights into the nutritional value of women or children), he insisted his paper's methods and calculations were valid.

'Taking into account lean tissue, fat and carbohydrates, we calculated the calorific value of the human body in the same way as in determining the energy value of beef, lamb or pork.'

In order of nutritional value, they had found male thighs and buttocks gave a beefy 15,500 calories, while the upper arms provided around 5450. The calves supplied about 6490 calories and the liver, 2570. The forearms and lungs each provided 1660. The kidneys together totalled 380 calories. The heart, barely a full single meal, came in at about 500.

Altogether, the meat on one adult male body would provide a tribe of, say, twelve people with only enough calories to survive for one day, 'about the same as a small seal or shark'. Whereas a Paleolithic bison would have offered them 600,000 calories, enough for ten days of food. And if they killed a mammoth, its 3.5 million calories would give them enough sustenance for two months.

'For our food value,' he concluded, 'we really aren't worth eating.'

The Reverend Isaac had been a less than nutritious fellow, Damian imagined. The two portraits of him in existence showed an austere-looking gent with wild eyebrows and mutton-chop whiskers. In defiance of the tropics, his several layers of English suiting (Isaac would have taken a lot of unwrapping before cooking) covered what looked like an angular, God-fearing body.

A grisly and gristly thought. More than ever, Damian found it difficult to take any of this seriously. But of course he was still curious. The 150th anniversary of Isaac Horne's death did mark the perfect time for a ceremony, and it would be the temperate season in Okina.

He foresaw gentle trade winds and azure seas and drinks under the palms. A holiday with an interesting edge. A Robinson Crusoe, Robert Louis Stevenson and Paul Gauguin sort of vacation.

*

Over the loudspeaker a voice gave an order in Pijin and the drumming and stamping stopped. Shadows were lengthening across the square and in the echoing silence each cannibal descendant now knelt before his assigned visitor, grasped his or her hands, groaned plaintively, roared into the sky, and burst into tears.

After several minutes of the islanders' wailing, while the embarrassed and anxious Horne descendants, some moved to tears themselves, patted the Okinans' heaving shoulders and attempted to soothe their distress, the loudspeaker barked another instruction. The islanders leapt to their feet, shook their heads to clear them, and recommenced the rhythmic puffing and stamping.

Now the loudspeaker blared again and the skeleton-men all sprinted aggressively towards the beach, growling theatrically and shouting war cries, and grabbing up clubs and battleaxes on their way.

All agape, the Hornes watched their wild progress across the sand. And there was more to see in the ocean. From around the headland waded another islander. Snappy waves and spindrift buffeted his makeshift nineteenth-century clothing. This fellow had a white painted face and stuck-on whiskers and as he splashed ashore he held aloft a big cardboard book emblazoned *BIBLE*.

Dashing into the shallows, a dozen armed and howling skeleton-men encircled him. Then, before the missionary's stunned great-great-great-grandchildren, amid much splashing and bloodcurdling yells, there followed a vigorous reenactment of the slaughter of the Reverend Isaac Horne.

*

As the skeleton-men carried the make-believe slaughtered Methodist ashore – soaked, cross and decidedly roughed up – the village chief, Tomasi Tetuani, the voice on the loudspeaker, appeared in the church doorway.

The crowd in the square parted before him. In traditional chieftain's grass skirt, head bowed and wiping away tears, the old man shuffled along the line of Hornes, handing each one a sperm whale's tooth, and kissing him or her on both cheeks. To each person he repeated, 'Isaac Horne died in this place because of us and we need to confess our past activities. I am the great-great-grandson of the chief who ordered his killing. It's time for repentance and to clear our consciences.'

Tendrils of smoke began drifting into the square at this point and the village dogs slunk towards the smell and sizzle of roasting meat. The Horne descendants frowned, a few chuckled uncertainly and nudged each other, and Lisa said, 'I hope they're not acting out the next part.'

'Relax, madam,' said the old chief. 'This is the twenty-first century.' He gestured towards the small stone church.

'We're Christians. Not Methodists like the Reverend Isaac, but Presbyterians, so near enough. In olden times many people were killed and eaten but we in this generation don't like it at all.'

And then a Land Rover pulled up in the square. Barefoot and fleshily bare-chested, though perfectly composed in his VIP grass skirt, George Bogenvanu emerged, embraced the chief, snatched up a microphone, and without further ado or introduction addressed the throng.

'What happened on this small island on that momentous day in 1867 was a clash of civilisations,' he declared, his rich voice filling the square. 'The old island gods and the battle club still ruled. Those who killed and consumed the Reverend Horne were not bad or vicious people. Our ancestors were simply honourable warriors who believed they were defending their home against threats to its established ways.'

From the row of Hornes, Jennifer Horne-Smith's voice rang out. 'Yes, absolutely!'

George Bogenvanu's eyes flicked in her direction before he continued. 'Today I come here to you by state-of-the-art twenty-first century technology, an Airbus H175 helicopter. I come from important Pacific Islands Forum meetings in major cities. From meetings discussing vital world matters like global warming and rising ocean levels.'

He paused and sighed deeply. 'Nevertheless, I take the time to observe old traditions' (here he slapped his broad, grass-skirted backside) 'and to make proper amends for a small, unfortunate but understandable moment in history.'

In the crowd some women began moaning and keening again. George Bogenvanu waved an avuncular hand in their direction before continuing.

'Their tears well from deep inside their hearts. Some of our people believe today's ceremony will lift the curse on Okina which they think has blighted their lives and is drowning our island. The curse that is rapidly sinking our home. They believe God has always looked down on us for killing a missionary. For clubbing him to death. For cutting up his body on that flat rock over there – the Isaac Horne Rock, as we call it. For roasting him and eating him.'

The Horne descendants all strained to see the Isaac Horne Rock, and Julie Truscott and Catherine Underhill exclaimed 'Oh my God!' and 'No!' and held their hands to their mouths. Light thunderclaps rolled over the mountains behind the village.

'That's why it was important for us to have this ceremony of reconciliation on this major anniversary.' George Bogenvanu was winding up now. 'Let me say we are deeply touched by your family's presence. I speak for all Okina in wishing you, the descendants of the Reverend Isaac Horne, the greatest joy of forgiveness as we finally end this historical disagreement. God bless you.'

Jennifer clapped vigorously, and the other Hornes, slowly at first, followed her example.

Did he actually apologise? Damian wondered.

*

At sunset the island women laid out a party on the beach: a feast of beef, pork, chicken, oysters and fish; of cassava, taro, yams, coconuts and heaped baskets of fruit; with coconut-shell bowls of kava and bottles of beer to drink, as well as Australian and New Zealand wines flown in with George Bogenvanu on the Pacific Islands Forum helicopter.

The trade winds blew more gently now, raucous birds began their night chorus in the palms, and the official party was ushered forward to sit in a circle on special cushions on the sand. As drinks were served, Bradley Horne got to his feet, with a little difficulty, and declared, 'Let us now toast the generous and kind people of Okina!'

Awkwardly, some clumsily standing, others sighing and half-rising before sinking down again, and some doggedly unmoving, the other Hornes raised their drinking utensils and repeated, 'To the people of Okina!' and Kevin Horne from Auckland, the oldest descendant, added loudly, 'Happy anniversary!'

Bradley Horne, a broadcaster on KEAR Christian Family Radio back in San Francisco, frowned and continued. 'I've always seen myself as following in Isaac's footsteps, and I believe that as good Christians we can now move on into the future. The past is the past. Sure, even a ritual killing seems wrong to us, and seeing where he died, where he was dismembered, *whew*. And, understandably, being cannibalised on top of that was always hard to accept . . .'

Kevin Horne interrupted with a laugh. 'We heard you Okinans even boiled his boots.'

Bradley cleared his throat, raised his voice and continued. 'But we've never borne any hatred to this village. Grandpa Isaac knew the risks when he came here. It's what happened in those days when good men tried to spread God's word. It was the island custom. But you folks have shown us great sympathy and kindness and Christian humility today.'

As thunder rolled again across the mountains, he paused theatrically. 'I'd like to think the coming rain is the sign of a new beginning. I feel the spirit of Isaac Horne is now at rest.'

George Bogenvanu clapped half-heartedly. Then, still traditionally bare-chested and barelegged, he adjusted his grass skirt, buttock-bumped Kevin Horne aside, and squeezed himself in between Lisa and Jennifer.

'It's not us that's stuck in the Dark Ages,' he muttered. 'With dirty fossil fuels. High-energy emissions.' He turned to Lisa. 'It thunders every evening. Believe me, there's no rain coming.'

*

Kevin Horne had begun the feast with a brave swig of kava before switching to beer. Now, nursing a glass of red wine, he was keen to share ancestor-data with distant family members.

'You others mightn't be aware that the New Zealand Hornes inherited some papers that Isaac delivered to the Royal Geographical Society. They detailed his earlier missions around these islands. On one occasion he counted thirty-five human jawbones hanging from a hut.'

Jennifer broke in. 'George, that was a wonderful ceremony,' she said. Her hand rested momentarily on his bare shoulder. 'You have a beautiful island.'

'This is like a dream,' Lisa offered.

'The Royal Geographical Society applauded his speech,' Kevin persisted. "Twenty smoke-dried human hands were hanging in the same house," Isaac told them. Outside, he'd counted eighty-five notches in a coconut tree. The natives told him each notch represented a human body they'd cooked and eaten there.'

George Bogenvanu looked up from his conversation with Lisa, sucked an oyster from its shell, then another. 'So that's what the savages told him?'

'Very long ago now,' Jennifer commented. 'On another planet.'

'Getting back to the boiled-boots business,' said Kevin, 'apparently after eating Isaac here on Okina, they cooked his boots too, and ate them with a vegetable called *bele*. Can you shed any light on that sacred habit?'

'Ha ha. *Bele*, also known as *slippery cabbage*. My favourite vegetable, *bele*. You're eating it now!' rumbled George Bogenvanu. 'But no Methodists' boots on the menu tonight. Or Methodists either, unfortunately.'

Then, to Jennifer's obvious displeasure, he ignored the rest of the party and focused his attention on Lisa.

*

Jennifer wasn't the only one rattled by George Bogenvanu's concentration on Lisa. Seated by his hosts on the other side of the festive beach circle from her, Damian naturally noticed another man's keen interest. Especially a huge, semi-naked, exotic and (in the circumstances) influential man. The master of this particular universe.

And his wife was hanging on this man's every word. Their heads were almost touching. Intimate. Meanwhile, Jennifer was now ostentatiously disregarding them. Nervily, she scrabbled through her bag, exclaimed 'Shit!' and asked a serving woman for a cigarette.

Damian, jealous and becoming angry, was struck by the helplessness that sometimes affected him on boats and islands. Even in his home city, at a party aboard a yacht on Sydney Harbour. Even on New Year's Eve. Especially on New Year's Eve. The realisation that you couldn't get off the boat if you wanted to. You couldn't leave. The same applied to islands. You had no control over events on an island. You were the dupe of whoever was in charge.

In this case, not until the bloody *Reef Explorer* picked them up tomorrow afternoon. Weather permitting.

Meanwhile, what was the protocol for disrupting a cannibal descendant's flirtation with the wife of a cannibal victim's descendant? As a civilised person, an honoured visitor (as the islanders insisted, despite his present cross-legged discomfort on the sand), what could he do?

And then chief Tomasi Tetuani, sitting beside him, leaned across and began peppering him with facts and figures on Pacific Islanders' superior football skills and overwhelming representation in the rugby teams of bigger nations, his hulking physique blocking Damian's view of Lisa and George Bogenvanu. And when he next looked, they were gone from the party.

A phrase, a sentence, loomed over Damian, and made his head throb. Words to do with the islanders' ceremony, words for their saying sorry, for making amends. The Okinans insisted on it:

There has to be an element of exchange.

*

The Horne family's accommodation was a tin-roofed and louvred guesthouse behind the church: separate male and female dormitories used for visiting Presbyterians and VIPs and, come election time, touring politicians.

Knowing no other place to look for Lisa, Damian made his way there, his mood worsened by Jennifer's bitter announcement as he'd left the party: 'If you're looking for your wife, she disappeared with George.'

'It's OK. They're just . . .' he began, and didn't know how to finish.

'Sure,' said Jennifer. 'Just a bit of cultural appropriation.'

The birds were silent now, the wind had dropped completely and he could hear the surf booming even louder on the reef. Flying foxes whirled and flapped over the village, and crabs scuttled across the square and over the church steps. The air smelled of fish and frangipanis.

The male dormitory was in shadow and there was no movement inside. On the beds were only the darker lumps of their travel luggage. In the female quarters, however, there were quiet voices and the glow of lamplight. He went up the steps and his wife and George Bogenvanu were there.

'This is Telei,' said Lisa, introducing a small girl of six or seven. 'Say hello. Her name means "precious". Tomorrow in another ceremony she'll be handed to you.'

She was smiling warmly and her hand was on the girl's hair. Damian had no conversation, on any level or on any subject. He and Lisa had no children of their own.

'We took a dear person from your family,' said George Bogenvanu. 'So we give you Telei, a dear person of ours, in exchange.'

'Not physically. A ceremonial gesture only,' Lisa said. 'Telei is an orphan with a serious case of the local eyesight problem. George told me all about her and her grim chances otherwise. I've said we'll accept responsibility for her treatment and education. We'll keep in touch with her.'

'In anything to do with cannibal compensation and reparations I always ask the wife,' said George Bogenvanu.

Black Lake and Sugarcane Road

After I spotted a python climbing into her picnic basket and yelled out, I got chatting to a young woman down at Black Lake. She had a badly scarred face and a baby. She flipped one of her sandals at the snake, casually backhand, like she was throwing a frisbee; the snake uncoiled itself from the basket and slid up the nearest camphor laurel, and we got talking.

Diamond pythons aren't venomous but it's still a conversation starter to find one nestled in your sandwiches, near a newborn baby and all, and we went on to discuss local snakes in general, especially the number of dangerous eastern browns around this summer.

'I hold the cane toad responsible,' I told her. 'It's their fault the snake ratio is out of whack.' I explained how before the toads migrated down here from Queensland, red-bellied black snakes used to keep the browns' numbers down by eating their offspring. But not only did the toads get a taste for young black snakes, the adult blacks liked to eat cane toads, and then they died from the toads' poison.

Sitting cross-legged on the grassy bank overlooking the lake, she seemed a typically serene Northern Rivers girl. Tumbling blond hair. Slender, tanned limbs. But under the hair her left cheek was shiny and crumpled like silver foil. The other side was pretty. While I tried not to stare at her scar, I outlined my theory and she nodded in an attentive way, brushed a bunch of hair aside and aimed the baby's mouth at a breast. The fontanelle began pulsating gently and the baby's ginger head fluff moved up and down as it nursed. It was a very new baby, still red and raw looking.

'End result,' I went on, 'fewer black snakes – venomous, but relatively shy with humans – and many more browns – highly venomous and aggressive.'

'That makes sense,' she said.

After our lengthy snake talk we introduced ourselves and I said, 'Do you mind,' and I sat down on the bank as well. 'I've been walking for two hours. Daily exercise.'

She said her name was Cynthia but she called herself China. 'So you've been to China?' I asked. 'Or maybe you admire Chinese things?'

She said *no* and *not particularly*. When she was little her father had called her China, as in rhyming slang: *China plate – mate.*

'We were very close, daddy and daughter. Then when I was twelve he went out for cigarettes one Saturday night, just like in a film, and never came back. He strolled off eating a Granny Smith apple.'

Ten years later she was working behind the bar in a Newcastle pub when her father came in. That was a shock. He saw her, downed his beer quickly and hurried off down Hunter Street. 'I didn't run after him. If that was his attitude, bugger him.' Of course he had a drink problem. He was a country-town pharmacist who could never remember whether he'd made up a prescription correctly. He couldn't trust himself and threw so much medicine down the sink that he went out of business.

China wasn't at all self-conscious about her naked breasts but she slanted her head so the non-scarred side was facing me. She said her baby daughter's name was Ayeshia, pronounced *Asia,* and she spelled it out. Keeping up the China connection, I guessed.

'We live down there on Sugarcane Road,' she told me, pointing south-west. Her partner Pete was part-managing a macadamia-nut farm for city investors: three Sydney surgeons needing a tax break. They didn't necessarily want a profit and were embarrassed that the nut price was going gangbusters at present. The Asians loved them.

'Pete's definitely growing only maccas these days,' she said firmly, switching the baby's head to the other breast. 'Not weed any more, not since the police crackdown.'

I said I'd heard of that. Helicopters and sniffer dogs, grumpy cops in riot gear tramping through the tropical rainforest, getting tangled up in the lawyer vines and spiky palms. Meanwhile bikers went unmolested and made ice in their backyard sheds.

She shook her head in wonderment and the scar glistened in the sunlight. 'Even the old pot establishment that made this area what it was, the pre-hydroponic guys, are under threat these days. Even cop-friendly blokes – old drinking mates, top surfers and footballers – are being arrested.'

The far bank of the lake was quivering in a heat mirage over Sugarcane Road so you couldn't tell where the lake ended and the cane fields began: a chequerboard plateau of sugarcane stretching to the horizon. An ibis stalked past and two purple swamp-hens scuttled along the shore.

'Your Pete's not being harassed then?' I asked. A bit impertinent of me, but age allows you that sort of presumption. By now I was wishing a good life for this frank, scarred girl. And her baby daughter, born in the wrong climate for a redhead.

'Not now. He did a lot of thinking and reading inside, and he's more into the natural life than ever. He's not a stoner any more, or a dealer. He's so obsessive these days it's not true, fighting the good fight against fluoridation of the water supply and child vaccinations, anything governmental. Every weekend he's out poisoning camphor laurels. You know that camphors are feral weeds that poison rivers and kill wildlife? Not to mention being bad for humans. They're not native Australian trees – they were introduced from Asia.'

'From China. And we're sitting in the shade of one now.'

She let that go. 'The camphors are the toxic enemy that Pete's sworn to eliminate. He says they even encourage drug use.' A flicker of irony showed on her face. 'Their thick canopies hide the crops from the police choppers.'

'He must have his work cut out.' The Northern Rivers landscape is enveloped and softened by millions of camphor laurels. Everywhere, the attractive rounded trees moderate the scenery. From the air the ground looks like the green European countryside of the model railway I had as a kid. At ground level the trees remind me of big bunches of broccoli. The camphors thrive where the cedar cutters and cattlemen razed the rainforest known as the Big Scrub in the nineteenth century. Farmers hate them because they shoot up everywhere. The hippies hate them because they're not native vegetation. They're ideologically unsound and not your noble Aussie eucalypts. Farmers and Greens in cahoots against a common enemy – a tree. That's one for the books.

While we watched a cormorant choking on an eel, I thought about little Ayeshia, still guzzling away on the breast. And of rubella, polio, meningococcal and tetanus, too, not to mention measles, mumps, whooping cough and diphtheria and the free government vaccinations that could prevent kids from catching them these days. And the daughter Margie and I lost to meningitis in 1984 – Emily. And then Margie going suddenly three months ago.

I'd never sleep if I didn't walk every day to tire myself out, to slow down the adrenaline. Around the lake takes me two hours at medium pace, then I dive in to cool off.

The cormorant gagged for about five minutes but eventually got the eel down. I was surprised the bird could even see an eel in Black Lake. Tea-trees dip into the lake and leach their tannin into the water. In the shallows it's yellow and warm and disconcertingly piss-coloured, but as you wade out the water turns orange, then quickly reddens to a deep burgundy. Dark as a blood test.

Twenty metres from shore the redness darkens to pitch black. By the time you're waist-deep you can't see the bottom. Then the lake bed falls sharply away. Who knows how deep the lake is now? The water temperature is layered, warmish for a metre or so down, then suddenly cold. Swimming overarm feels threatening if you have your eyes open. I swim backstroke so I don't have the sensation of swimming into an abyss. If you were drowning or slipped under on purpose your body would be hard to find. I've occasionally given it some thought.

Strange how this weird soft water doesn't sting your eyes, and your skin feels smooth when you get out. Then you forget what it was like out in the deep. How pessimistic it made you feel.

A dusty white Toyota HiLux pulled up sharply then, and a burly red-bearded fellow got out and strode over. He wore a black cap with a motor-oil logo and sunglasses perched on top of it. 'There you are!' he said, half-smiling and frowning simultaneously, and squatted down beside us. 'It's getting bloody late, China. I wondered where you'd got to. Off with one of the old boyfriends maybe.'

'Sorry, babe. I took Ayeshia for a walk to the lake and this gentleman saved us from a diamond python.'

I'm not sure I like younger people nowadays referring me to as a *gentleman* or *sir*. It's all to do with age. Until I was fifty I wasn't *sir.* I was *mate*. On that subject, I was surprised now at Pete's age. He had twenty or twenty-five years on China. There was grey in the red beard. We shook hands. He applied pressure. Not a particularly friendly handshake.

'Pythons are fucking harmless,' Pete scoffed. 'Unless you're a rat or a rabbit. Or the family cat. Jesus, I thought everyone knew that.'

'I know, babe. I was joking. The snake crawled into our basket so I scared it up that tree.'

He glared at the tree for a long moment, went to his truck, and returned with a poster and a staple gun. He nailed the poster to the tree: a skull and crossbones and a scarlet slogan. *Stop the Camphor Menace.*

'I'll come back later for that one,' he said.

'China says the tree-poisoning keeps you pretty busy,' I said to him. 'How do you go about it?'

He frowned at me, then her, and didn't speak for some seconds. Then he focused his eyes on me. A fierce faded blue. He blinked.

'To answer your question, it depends on the site, tree size, access and your personal herbicide preference. There's various methods – cut stump, stem injection, basal bark or foliar spray techniques. All legal herbicides available to any weekend gardener. Glyphosate 360, picloram 100, triclopyr 300. Just doing my bit to disrupt plant cell growth. Someone has to, when the government does bugger all.

He turned abruptly from me to China. 'Fun's over. Time to go. I'm fucking hungry.' He stomped ahead to the truck.

The sun was above the far cane fields. Still about an hour from setting. As she packed up the baby and the basket, China murmured, 'He likes to eat early, drink a bit and hit the sack.'

Then she said, 'You were wondering about my scar?'

Of course I had been, amongst other things. Like life in Sugarcane Road. But I muttered, 'Not at all. I'm sorry I've kept you.'

'It's OK,' she said, and touched my arm. 'Actually, it wasn't him that time. It was one of my exes.'

Paleface and the Panther

At one time I saw Anthony only as a potential portrait subject, his looks and manner interestingly weird to a painter. Back then his skin was so white and translucent you could see the veins fanning out from his temples into his rusty curls. The vulnerability of those electric-blue wires was remarked upon by total strangers. Old ladies on the bus tut-tutted about him. Sometimes his skull looked like a physiology poster. At the same time, the eggshell frailty of an orphanage or illness seemed to cling to his body. When he had his shirt off for the bath or the beach – for the few seconds before he was wrapped protectively in pyjamas or long-sleeved, sun-safe swimwear – there were those eerie neon veins again, beaming out from inside his chest.

I'd tried to paint him six or seven times, but never with any success. I find children difficult in any case. They come out either sentimentally cherubic or Hollywood demonic. In Anthony's case, especially in oils, he looked like a gnome or a changeling, with a wily fairytale face. And of course I couldn't resist the veins – maybe I overdid the cobalt. Not surprisingly, the paintings met with strong disapproval from Liz, Anthony's mother, who'd probably had Renoir and innocence and velvet suits in mind, and she destroyed them before I could reuse the canvases.

Even in real life Anthony didn't seem like a normal West Australian boy to me back in the eighties. Not either tanned or sunburnt, not freckled or peeling, more like a vitamin- and protein-deprived Irish waif from yesteryear. *Just off the boat,* as they used to say. But he wasn't sick or poor, just pallid and thin. And he was actually a fifth-generation Australian, a McMahon, and only half-orphaned, and when a temperamental Irish flush masked his veins, and his curls were unravelling in the summer humidity, he was the image of our father.

Christ, our lunch today in Fremantle reminded me of Anthony's tenth birthday party, not a day I particularly wanted to remember, and a cricket game in a Peppermint Grove park of buffalo grass sloping down to the river, a match the birthday boy had insisted on, where he'd just been clean-bowled for the third time in a row.

It was torture to watch. Anthony was trying out his new Slazenger cricket set, my present to him. A cricket bat, ball, pads, gloves, stumps and bails that came in a nifty PVC bag with the Slazenger panther emblem leaping in full horizontal stretch the length of the bag.

It was bloody expensive, much more than I'd normally spend, but I wanted to give him something sporty and manly, something we could occasionally do together and maybe shift the gender balance a little. Make him not so milky pale and veiny. Anthony was always surrounded by women and I felt vaguely guilty for not having paid him more attention when I was living it up. Painting pretty hard, yes, but also playing hard. The usual recreational activities. Anyway, if Anthony's flushed cheeks and boisterous eagerness to test the cricket set were anything to go by, he loved the gift.

Over and again he was clean-bowled but refused to leave the crease. Even as he flailed around, his glowering, determined face – our father again – seemed to say, 'Are you all mad? Why should I go out? What idiot would swap batting for bowling or, even more ludicrously, fielding? Batting is the whole point, isn't it?' It was *his* birthday and *his* new cricket set and *he* was the most important person here, especially today of all days.

Not surprisingly, the twenty or so other kids, the party guests fielding in the park that January afternoon, soon lost concentration and patience. The birthday boy had been allowed to bat first. Uncle Jason was bowling underarm, we'd substituted a tennis ball for the hard cricket ball, and Jason had bowled him out three times already.

All over the park, young fielders were flopping down on the ground and sucking twigs and peppermint leaves and peering longingly towards the river and the party table that Anthony's mother and aunts were setting up under the peppermint trees.

The kids had given up on having a turn with the bat and now they wanted to swim or eat: at this rate there'd soon be an uprising. Oblivious to the general restiveness, the three Kennedy sisters were drinking their customary spritzers and laughing while they blew up balloons and tied them to the trees, special balloons that said *Happy 10th Birthday Anthony!*

I was wicketkeeping. I wanted him to succeed, and I wanted the cricket set to be an appreciated gift, so I gave him a bit of leeway. But eventually I said, 'You're really out, my man. Give someone else a turn.'

He swung at another slow underarm ball from Jason, and missed again. I trudged uphill after the ball while he thumped the grass in frustration. He still didn't give up the bat.

Unusually for a Perth summer afternoon the sea breeze hadn't yet arrived and the day gave off a sullen chalky glare that stung the eyes. In the river below us, other shrieking children were bombing and diving off the jetty – non-party guests having a much better time – and becalmed yachts lolled in a deep-water bay as smooth as oily glass. Ageless Impressionist subject matter. You've also spotted the summer scene in a hundred atmospheric newspaper photographs: skinny show-off boys caught midair, urchins spreadeagled between jetty and water.

Even at my age I envied them. Already my shirt was sticking to me from all that trudging after the missed balls. The buffalo grass had an annoying way of gripping the ball and stopping it from rolling back down to me.

'Don't be a bad sport,' I told him. I was feeling disheartened as well as hot. Birthday Boy was ruining the party mood. As I threw the ball back to Jason, I told him, 'Don't bowl any more until the spoilsport walks.'

Jason looked for direction to the women with the spritzers and balloons. In the shade of the peppermint trees the Kennedy sisters had taken off their sunhats, revealing three different hues of red hair in gradations from vivid orange peel to mercuric sulphide pigment to dark rust. They all had cigarettes going too, which interfered with their balloon-blowing efforts, and every now and then one of the women would gasp and giggle and her half-inflated balloon would escape, spinning, blurting and farting crazily over their heads.

Liz, the dark-rusty one, my stepmother, glanced at us. 'I hope you've got sunscreen on, Ant,' she said.

Jason looked back at me uncertainly. 'Show him again how to hold the bat.'

Jesus, Jason was being avuncular. He was twenty-eight, married to the youngest Kennedy sister, Jeanette, and in our occasional dealings the five years he had over me seemed to give him the advantage. But in the matter of Anthony, I felt I had the upper hand. Jason was only Anthony's uncle by marriage, and even less related to me, not my family at all. Anyway, I had deaths on my side. Two deaths gave me the edge.

'Here we go again,' I said. I gripped Anthony's narrow shoulders and spun him side-on to the bowler. The panther emblem was stamped on the bat as well. I twisted the bat handle around in his hands.

'This is your last ball,' I said. 'Keep a straight bat. See that panther on the bat? It should face your right leg. Defend your wicket. Take it easy. Don't swing like a dunny door.'

He squirmed free of my hands and shuffled back to his incorrect stance. If he swung the bat from there he'd not only miss the ball again but knock his wicket over. He eyes had an oddly familiar shine. My father's old Dewar's glint, his Johnnie Walker midnight-aggressive glint. 'Go shit-fuck-shit away!' Anthony growled. 'I don't have to take any notice of you!'

My God, he needed a smack. 'That's not even proper swearing, Paleface,' I said as I walked off.

*

When I arrived at the restaurant, an outdoor seafood place in the Fremantle fishing harbour, he was already seated. An unusual choice for Anthony, I thought: not fashionable but overly marine-themed, with a table of bluff Yorkshire accents and porky pink skins on one side of us, a tidy arrangement of Japanese on the other. There was the usual network of wires strung above the tables to discourage seagulls and several pleading *Please Don't Feed the Birds* signs. Of course the tourists were ignoring these deterrents and hurling their chips into the harbour, where diving and wheeling gulls enjoyed uninterrupted and raucous access.

I'd suggested the lunch at my stepmother's behest. 'What's he doing with his life?' Liz moaned. 'Can you find out and give him some advice, put him right?' According to her, Anthony had abruptly left Alison and their two children, tossed in his partnership with Fairhall Burns Corrie, turned vegetarian, and was 'living with some hippie witch in a mud hut up in the hills'.

I imagine she thought I was more in tune with arty, low-life ways. Painting and bohemia and all that. Anthony's spinning-out sounded like an early midlife crisis to me, a middle-class cliché, but at this stage Liz was phoning me in tears every day with news of Anthony's latest New Age transgression.

'He's killing me. I don't understand him any more. He's acting all superior to everyone, angry and touchy-feely at the same time. The hippie witch must have some eerie power over him.'

I heard deep raspy breaths; she was drawing heavily on a cigarette and even over the phone she sounded old and needy. I pictured the almost-empty bottle of chardonnay close by.

'What's all this guru stuff, anyway?' she went on. 'Numerology, astrology, holistic blah-blah, tantric mumbo jumbo. A 37-year-old lawyer doesn't need all this hoo-ha. I certainly don't need all this hoo-ha! Bruce would be rolling in his grave. What are we going to do?'

We? I didn't need any hoo-ha either. But I felt sorry for Liz. She was no evil storybook stepmother. Sally and I had hardly begrudged her marrying our father. She hadn't pinched him from Monica, our mother: Bruce had been a widower, after all. And for a few years after Mum died we were sort of numb, and kept to ourselves while Dad grieved alone and left us to our own devices. Then, as a widowed parent herself – after his death five years later – she'd always been amiably haphazard and not the least bit maternal.

I think that's why we didn't overly resent her when we were younger; she wasn't vying for our love. Sally and I had each other and it suited us that she was affectionately distant, not in competition with our mother over anything, and allowed our sad reverence for her to remain undisturbed.

Her focus was completely on Bruce, her husband whether alive or dead. As soon as Anthony was seven, she'd sent him off to boarding school, to Aquinas. She'd married late, at forty, the eldest Kennedy sister and the last to go, and for the fact of being married at all she was grateful to Bruce every day. If he was no longer there, she wanted to be alone with his memory – his memory and the remains of his wine cellar.

But *we*? What could I do? Anthony was a grown man and, by Perth's standards, already a successful one: a commercial lawyer, yachtsman, weekend tennis player, and the owner of two storeys of heritage sandstone, a pool, a tennis court behind a disciplined plumbago hedge and, from the second-floor bedrooms at least, three river glimpses and a misty view of the Darling Range. He was responsible for his own actions.

Anyway, maybe he was doing the right thing. I was sorry for his kids, but Alison was a provincial Anglophile snob with a cleanliness obsession. The sort who washed my beer glass the minute I set it down, who made me feel unkempt and grubby in her company. Maybe Anthony had seen the light.

How would I describe our half-brother relationship? We were like longtime acquaintances. Beyond our father we had little in common. Our political views collided. Anthony was conservative and well-off, and I was neither. He was a law graduate and I was basically self-educated. There was a fourteen-year age difference and no physical resemblance. Whenever we met up, at Christmas or other family gatherings, we didn't converse so much as banter and nod agreeably and top up each other's drinks.

'How's the art world?' he'd ask. 'Selling any?' He came to my exhibitions because he liked the business-social aspect, plus the chance to mingle safely with a few raffish characters.

Always we acted as brothers. But we were acting. We weren't exactly brothers, and we weren't exactly friends. We were something in between.

But this was an intriguing twist, being called on for advice. Until recently the role of the family bohemian, the black sheep, had been mine.

*

Even his handshake was different now, loose and metallic. All those silver rings on his fingers. Another in his left ear. Silver bracelets on each wrist, a necklace of little beads and seeds and stones, and another thin chain with some sort of gemstone pendant banging portentously against his sternum.

I'd never seen an ornamented Anthony before – the Old Aquinian cufflinks used to be his limit. Add the rumpled natural fibres, a collarless shirt, rubbery sandals (no leather in evidence), floppy drawstring trousers like pyjama pants that didn't reach his ankles, and he'd gone the whole hog, sartorially. Guru-wear, his mother called it. It looked more like grandpa-wear to me – if your grandpa was institutionalised and had got into Grandma's jewellery box.

I'd dressed up in a shirt with a collar and, for the first time, I felt like the conservative brother. 'So, what's happening, Ant?' I said as I sat down. The *what's happening* came out more abruptly than I'd intended. I meant it more as *How's it going, bro?* But it came out like *What the Christ are you doing with your life*?

'What do you mean?'

To be honest, he looked well. He'd lost the extra weight he'd stacked on, and those childhood veins had long since vanished into ruddy cheeks and freckled temples.

'What's doing?' What are you up to?'

His frown at least was familiar. His cutlery caught a sunray as he was arranging his knife and fork at right angles to the table edge.

'I heard you'd gone vegetarian. So you eat fish then?'

Yes, he ate fish. Apparently his new lifestyle didn't preclude alcohol either, or his liking for good wines, and once the bottle he'd ordered arrived he began to open up.

'Look, I've embarked on a new journey.' His fingers were still fiddling with the tableware. 'Everything in my life has been leading me to this point.'

'Doesn't it always?' I said. But I was trying to be understanding. 'Tell me about your life changes. Who's the girlfriend? Do I know her?' There was a fair chance I did. My gravelly three acres of banksias and grass trees were also up in the hills. 'Are you sure you're doing the right thing?'

Part calming-Jesus, part-lawyer, he raised an admonishing hand. 'Let me show you something.' He held up the wine bottle, pointed to its label, read out its name: *Torbreck Roussanne Marsanne. Barossa Valley.* Its design featured two concentric circles. He tapped them with a be-ringed finger. His expression, both legal and wisdom-of-the-ages, declared *I rest my case.*

'What?'

'The label says it all. It's a personal message to me. It tells me I'm doing the right thing.'

'Really?' I toyed with the idea of the Torbreck wine people not only knowing of his existence but basing their graphic designs and marketing strategies around his changing emotions. 'I thought the label was saying "Please buy this wine".'

Anthony sighed and cast his eyes around the restaurant. 'The thing is, I can get confirmation anywhere,' he said. 'OK, see those napkin rings on the buffet over there?' Two silver circles stood side by side, intersecting slightly. 'They're speaking to me. They're confirming the rightness of my journey.'

'Do the circles represent you and the new woman?'

He sighed. 'Among other things.'

'Are you going to tell me her name?'

'Does it matter? Sarita. Maya. Parissa. She goes by several names. She's the essential, fundamental woman.'

Fundamental woman. I got the picture.

He said, 'It's not sex, if that's what you're thinking.'

Our plates of snapper arrived then, the fish engulfed by circles of beetroot and orange slices and onion and pineapple rings. Collage as much as meal. As I scraped the bright geometric toppings off my fish I almost asked whether all this round food was conveying wisdom to him.

I was running out of questions, and Anthony, his cheeks already flushed from the alcohol and conversation, was still frowning. I swallowed another mouthful of wine. I was forced to raise my voice over the dour northern English voices and seagull squawks.

So, this new life journey, one of tossed-in job and dumped family – apparently a celibate journey, to boot – was being determined by serviette rings and wine labels.

'Ant, I think you need to see someone,' I said.

*

Charged with carbohydrates, the melee of kids fled the debris of the party table. For several minutes Jason and I tried to exhaust them by organising a game of Red Rover under the peppermint trees, but the idea didn't take hold.

Weary of manners and adult directions, first one boy then another broke away from the game and began running up the hill and rolling down again. Soon all of them were rolling and shrieking and somersaulting down the slope. Late-afternoon shadows were stretching across the park but the day's clamminess seemed to have increased. In the heat, with the river so close, this fierce prickly game looked like madness. Over and over, hysterical, they rolled and climbed.

Behind the main clump of boys, Anthony, less quick and agile, dizzy and red-faced, grass sticking to his clothes, picked himself up and staggered up the incline once more. His legs were wobbly sticks. As he climbed, he had to avoid the mob of boys tumbling down, and several times he was knocked over. He was no longer in charge of events and the rebellious horde ignored his angry protests and indignant arm-waving. That urgent noise he was making sounded somewhere between shouting and sobbing. Then he got to his feet halfway up the hill, beat his sides with his fists and started to scream.

*

Anthony drained his glass, leaned back in his chair, dropped his hands in his lap, breathed deeply – once, twice – as if willing the dangerous glimmer in his eyes to fade and a suitably serene expression to slide down his cheeks.

'See someone? You mean a shrink?'

'Well, a psychologist or counsellor or whatever.' It sounded lame. He'd lost his father at the age of five. I tended to forget that. I'd been twelve when Mum died and eighteen when Dad did. Being five was probably worse. But at least he still had a mother. 'You might find it helpful, dealing with old emotional stuff.'

'I have my own spiritual mentors,' he declared. 'And I've never been more emotionally stable in my life. In fact, I'm so calm I don't even resent your bloody gratuitous advice.'

'Just because you're calm doesn't mean you're not fucked up and don't need help.'

'And you'd be competent to judge that. With your background? A fucking painter who didn't even go to university?'

'Someone with more life experience and common sense than you, brother.'

He raised an eyebrow. The resemblance was extraordinary. It could have been our father, towards the end. When he was bitter and hitting the bottle late at night and always giving Sally and me strange looks; when he realised he'd remarried too soon, the wrong woman; when he was still mourning my mother Monica.

'*Brother*? Are you sure?'

'Jesus! Well, half-brother then.'

He was running a finger around the rim of his wineglass so it made that irritating thin scream. Another bloody circle. 'You're sure of that?' he repeated.

I could have whacked his smug hippie-lawyer head. 'What are you getting at?'

His smile was suddenly prim, as if an old score was finally being settled. 'You've never wondered why you're short and olive-skinned? How incurious can you be? I hate to be the one to pass on family secrets, but did you know Monica couldn't have children?'

For a few seconds I couldn't see. The glare off the harbour, snowy tablecloths, the swirling white ruckus of the seagulls blinded me. The whole scene was leached of tint and shade. Strangely, I recalled the faint watercolours of Lloyd Rees when his sight was fading at the end of his painting life. If it were me, I'd have chosen brighter and brighter colours. But his were pale, soft yet urgent paintings that paralleled his life force. Paintings needing to be quickly said before time ran out.

I remembered how stressful my sister always found those get-togethers of the gingery Kennedys. The insouciant ways of the Spritzer Sisters, as she called them, the blithe patronising attitude of Liz's siblings towards 'Monica's kids' made Sally edgy and self-conscious in their presence, and savagely mocking later. My shy sister always got plenty of sardonic material from family gatherings but they wore her out and in the end she'd given up attending them. My older, smaller sister.

'Very commendable of Monica and Dad in the circumstances

to take you both in,' Anthony said. 'I guess it must have been spiritually fulfilling in its way to snatch you from the tribe. A tent boxer at the Royal Show, your father. Your mum was a little white fourteen-year-old whose dad ran the Ferris wheel and wasn't too thrilled with the outcome. Not sure of Sally's background – much the same, I reckon.'

Anthony rolled his napkin into a ball. 'Anyway it was all Monica's doing, the adoptions, so I've been told, and Dad went along with them because of her infertility problems. Complex legal processes involved, health and cultural risks. Made everything easier all round, you two being quite pale, I guess. God knows *your* community doesn't give up its waifs too readily.'

*

Some of the boys on the hill stopped surging and somersaulting to stare at Anthony and his noise. The sisters glanced up from their spritzers and cigarettes, shook their heads wearily and resumed chatting.

Anthony bellowed on. Tired of the hubbub, a couple of boys made for the shade, brushed themselves down, drank some Coke and looked around for entertainment. Then they spotted the Slazenger bag, unzipped it, got out the bat and ball, set up the stumps and began quietly playing.

I joined the game behind the wicket. The bowler bowled properly overarm, using the regulation hard six-stitcher; the batsman struck the ball squarely back to him two, three times. The face of the bat and the panther emblem hit the ball correctly with sharp, efficient cracks.

Down the hill thundered Anthony. His pallor was gone and his curls were damp and stringy. Muddy tear streaks ran down his cheeks and spit frothed on his lips.

'Give everything to me!' he yelled. He raced up to the surprised batsman and snatched the bat from him; he took the ball from the bowler. He grabbed up the stumps. From the bitter ferocity of his glare, I could tell he thought I'd betrayed him.

'What are you doing?' I said.

From under the peppermint trees his mother sang out, 'Ant, play nicely.'

For a moment he stood there undecided, with the cricket gear clasped possessively to his chest. Then he stacked it back into the Slazenger bag, picked up the bag and marched off across the park. He'd gone maybe twenty metres when something apparently occurred to him and he stopped, returned to the party table, collected all his birthday presents – some gifts still unopened – and crammed them into the bag as well. It was a tight squeeze: the panther was stretched to bursting.

Very businesslike then, a grim smile on his face, he strode down to the river. I watched him go, just as grimly. The sea breeze had finally arrived, sweeping through the peppermint trees, and snappy little waves began breaking on the shore. I followed him but I wasn't going to stop him. Surely this tantrum would soon play itself out.

Indeed, the bag must have become heavy because he had to haul it the last few metres across the sand and on to the jetty. Brushing aside skylarking wet children, curious onlookers, he dragged it the length of the jetty until he came to a pontoon just above the deep water. Then he heaved the bag into the river.

All that wood inside it, and the trapped air; it floated easily. A couple of children dived in and set off after it, then gave up. The tide was going out and the Slazenger bag sailed away into the bay and bobbed into the wide river estuary. I reached the pontoon, and sat down along from Anthony, and we watched the bag in silence until it was gone.

Varadero

Checking into Varadero's oldest hotel, the Internacional, Alex and Amanda were mildly surprised to be welcomed in the foyer by three larger-than-life statues of a golden mermaid, a Venus de Milo and a plump naked woman who seemed to be expressing breast milk into a pineapple.

In a Cuban beachscape of flashy resorts, the Internacional was down to two stars these days, and lucky to have them. But Frank Sinatra, Ava Gardner and significant Mafia figures and Caribbean dictators were said to have caroused here. To Alex and Amanda, such a raffish history was definitely worth a couple of stars.

Enthusiasts of singular and colourful travel destinations, the couple had been impressed by TripAdvisor's review of the hotel. 'Admittedly ageing nowadays,' TripAdvisor declared, 'Cuba's first beach-resort hotel, situated between the Bay of Cárdenas and the Florida Straits, on the lushly vegetated Peninsula de Hicacos, was opened to loud fanfare and wild Batista-era revelry in 1950.'

Despite an abstract interest in old Fidel, still apparently clinging to life in some secret hospice, and Amanda's wistful nostalgia for dashing young Che, killed more than ten years before she was born but commemorated on her T-shirt, there was something deliciously wicked about the phrase 'wild Batista-era revelry', with its connotations of vice, corruption and tyranny. Even sixty-five years later.

At the reception desk they kept nudging each other. Alex indicated the bosomy woman with the pineapple. 'Our Lady of Perpetual Lactation?'

'Goddess of the pina colada?' Amanda wondered.

The decor! The foyer of overstuffed leather couches and gold-framed mirrors! The walls painted in whirligig patterns of turquoise, pink, green and brown! '*Mad Men* meets Caribbean bordello!' Amanda said. This was by no means a criticism.

Check out the framed faded photographs of those early carousers! Yes, there were Frank and Ava. Notice Frank's askew bow tie and Ava's tipsy, smoky eyes! Look at the tables and banquettes of despots and mobsters! What with all those cunning, grinning faces smoking cigars and drinking champagne – all the shrewd Mafiosi and gold-toothed presidents ogling hot beauties in strapless gowns – it was impossible to tell oligarch from politician, ruler from racketeer.

And – the couple was delighted to think – in the racy and spicy Internacional, here we are as well: Alex and Amanda Emerson from Melbourne. They were now actually in rebellious, defiant, glamorous, other-worldly Cuba. *Travellers* though, rather than *tourists*. They hated the word, the very idea, of *tourist*, with its connotations of castles and cathedrals and tour buses full of geriatrics.

All the way from inner-city Melbourne to Sydney, to Dallas/Fort Worth. Then, because of the ridiculous US flight restrictions, via a roundabout stopover in Panama City to Havana. And from Havana by local bus to Varadero. They could hardly believe their own adventurous natures.

Of the Internacional's three elevators only the narrow service lift behind the kitchen was working. It smelled of lard and rum and stale body odour. It was another trek to their fourth-floor room, along a worn and stained red carpet that squelched underfoot in places and occasionally revealed holes in the cement floor through which they could see the floor below.

But they smiled as they pointed out to each other the corridor's more blatant safety risks and structural shortcomings – the gaping floor cavities, bare pipes and exposed electric wires – and made humorous gagging faces at the miasma of mould, rum and pork grease that rose from downstairs to meet the stench of cigars filling the corridor.

None of this bothered them. On the contrary, they were already plotting an exotic holiday narrative for their more conservative and timid friends, people like Matt Irvine and Sue Millett and the Pepworths, for whom the idea of Cuba was too unsettling to ever consider visiting. People for whom travel meant France and Italy and Spain. And Britain, yet again. At a pinch, Hungary and Croatia.

Already the Internacional was providing great anecdotal material. That neat hole in the window of their room, for instance. In the retelling, a bullet hole, naturally. And while the whirring and cavernous air conditioner indicated thirty degrees celsius, the temperature was more like thirteen and sent an unchangeable narrow but fierce wind stream directly onto the bed.

The bed. Already they'd chosen to believe this was Frank and Ava's room back in 1950. So this must have been Frank and Ava's bed: an important potential story point, with the image of Frank and Ava cavorting here already dominating the couple's imaginations.

The bed was king-size. But the compulsory air blast, the disturbing hospital-style pink rubber sheet on top of the mattress, the two single-bed sheets running horizontally, and the two thin, hard pillows rather negated thoughts of Frank and Ava's shenanigans. The window had no curtains, but it opened onto the sparkling ocean, as stunning as its publicity, so this lapse was easily forgiven, too.

Varadero. Alex liked saying the word. Rolling it around his tongue. Varadero retained the Batista-era feel. A Cuban cultural warp: for capitalist countries an inexpensive beach resort, with its own airport offering easy access from Europe and Canada. As it turned out, a place of minimal locals and many overweight, heavy-smoking Europeans in scanty beachwear.

They couldn't believe its languid voraciousness. Once you'd checked into the hotel and paid the tariff upfront, all food and drinks were free, twenty-four hours a day. Encouraged to refill their thermoses of mojitos, pina coladas or beer whenever they wanted, drunken guests proliferated: shrieking women and booming men. Germans, English, Spaniards, Canadians, Italians,

French, Russians. All of them smoking through their meals, and everywhere else as well. Naturally, the men ostentatiously puffed on Havana cigars.

On the beach terrace, amplified salsa and *son* interspersed with vintage sentimental American pop songs began playing at nine a.m. and continued until midnight. A cloud of greasy smoke, thick enough to coat the throat, wafted from the hotel's free hamburger-and-chips bar and hung over the terrace all day, mingling with the sweet grease of the guests' suntan lotions.

The guests. On their first morning, beckoned by the white beach and the serene dreamy sea, Alex and Amanda were almost bowled over by guests scurrying with their drink casks to grab a plastic deckchair that wasn't broken. Chairless, the couple wandered seawards, past more statues of gods, goddesses and Mesoamerican heroes, most missing a nose or an arm or two, that frowned out across the sea. Maybe towards America.

Once beach territory was established and the first drinks of the day consumed, a sort of glistening torpor seemed to strike the guests. Males of all ages languidly sunbaked, strolled and blatantly posed, baring shiny, shaved bodies in tight, bulge-enhancing trunks. Regardless of their years and shapes, the women all wore bikinis.

Rather than submerge their bodies in this dazzling sea, however, men and women alike ventured only knee-deep. Motionless as sentinels, they raised their faces and chests to the sun, chins held high, their heads and torsos and swimsuits carefully kept dry, before returning to the sand to refill their drink flasks, apply more body oil, and fry once more.

Amanda dived in first and Alex quickly joined her. To their surprise when they surfaced and glanced around the shallows, they were the only guests actually swimming. But how delicious it was after their long journey to stretch out and stroke through this temperate, glassy sea of exotic history.

To active travellers like these two, who'd previously clambered from inflatables onto Antarctic ice floes, trekked through Mugabe's Zimbabwe and, most recklessly of all, nightclubbed in Bogotá, to be staying at a scenic foreign beach and not to sample its ocean was incomprehensible – almost a crime. The other non-swimming, sun-obsessed Varadero vacationers were letting the side down. Like the noisy, overweight and sunburned family nearby, for example, whose lobster-skinned matriarch slammed down her drink flask, hitched up her bikini bottoms and yelled, 'Shit, I've got to pee again!'

Not the behaviour of a bone fide traveller, someone who appreciated the offerings of their destination. Nor did the swimwear of another beachgoer pass Alex and Amanda's traveller-test. This thin, melancholy man trudged across the sand before them. He was trussed up in a purple swimsuit that clung to his groin in a genital sling, rose up his bony chest, parted his bony buttocks in the back, and looped around his neck.

They'd never seen such a bizarre garment. 'It's a mankini,' murmured Amanda.

They saw the mankini man each day of their stay. Stoop-shouldered and middle-aged, his long hair streaked with blond highlights, he arrived at the beach at noon, always followed by a muscular black Cuban youth walking several paces behind him.

Each day the two males sat on the same patch of sand, the young man, a sullen chain-smoker, always keeping a distance of several metres between them, and appearing to ignore the other. The downhearted man in the mankini would take a drink or two and, every so often, walk slowly into the sea. He'd stand thigh-deep for ten or fifteen minutes and gaze forlornly at the horizon. Then he'd return to the sand, roll down the top of his extraordinary swimsuit, bare his hollow chest to the sun, and light two cigarettes.

Passing one to his unenthusiastic companion, he'd nonchalantly, optimistically, lean towards the boy, putting his hand on his knee as he did so. There was no conversation between them. Without speaking, the boy would take the fresh cigarette and move out of reach again.

*

The next night Amanda spotted the mankini man and the Cuban boy eating in the hotel restaurant and nudged Alex. Until then another diner, a dangerous-looking Central American woman in a gold bra and shimmering gold hotpants, had claimed their dinnertime attention and a certain mention in their travel narrative.

Dining with her sleek husband and two chubby children, all solemnly munching their way through fried pork chunks and plantain chips, the woman stared silently at her family throughout the meal. Mama let her eyes fall on each of them in turn: first the husband and then the two boys. Under her glare they dropped their eyes and kept eating, munching pork and swigging Coke. Throughout the meal no one spoke. She held her knife like a weapon, first stabbing the food and then eating off the knife, sliding the blade slowly through her scarlet lips.

'Happy families,' said Alex.

'I bet hubby can't wait to get home,' Amanda said.

And suddenly the family finished eating and was gone, and in the gap opened in the dining room by their absence, Amanda noticed the mankini man and the Cuban youth. Again they were together but still ostensibly separate, sitting at neighbouring tables while keeping up the myth of discreteness.

Again they weren't speaking. Each separately and silently helped himself from the buffet. The melancholy thin man scarcely succumbed to the food on offer and then picked dispiritedly at his meagre meal, but the boy piled his plate with the *ropa vieja*, the rice, the plantains, the beans, the pork chunks, the sliced pork sausage and the pork mince, ate ravenously and returned to the buffet twice more.

While the thin man tentatively sipped a Cristal beer and gazed unhappily about the room, the boy drank two Cokes, belched into his fist, his eyes never leaving his plate.

'What's their story, I wonder?' Amanda murmured.

Alex said, 'Pretty obvious, wouldn't you say?'

'Well, yes. But they don't seem to get on very well.'

'Just a business transaction. And the boy is ashamed.'

*

Alex and Amanda didn't wish to swim next morning. A strong wind had sprung up overnight and a choppy sea snapped on the shore and carried beach chairs into the sea. The Caribbean was transformed into petulant whitecaps and sand and spray blew against their bedroom window and wind whistled through the bullet hole in the glass.

It was hard to imagine Frank and Ava nestled down in the Internacional today, with doors and shutters banging, and guests complaining loudly about the weather, and beach conditions so blustery that Alex and Amanda decided to spend the day in town.

Despite their dislike of tourist habits, Amanda was not beyond buying a souvenir or two. Not souvenirs, she insisted, just *gifts,* presents for friends and family. Actually, she enjoyed markets more than she let on, and Che Guevara's ubiquitous presence in every market stall – the interesting unkempt beard, the jaunty angle of the beret, the same thoughtfully virile frown into the middle distance – encouraged her to buy two more Che T-shirts, a Che belt buckle, a Che coffee mug and a set of Che salad servers.

To Alex's and her surprise, however, the constant appearance of Che's image in the Varadero markets was matched by many caricatures of black Cubans. A grinning, fat-lipped Sambo and bandana-wearing, massively hipped Mammy were comically represented in every market stall, in tacky souvenirs of every sort, from ashtrays to bottle openers. Even in the stalls run by black shopkeepers.

This was unsettling. Back home, as they said to each other, indeed in any Western country, such caricatures would be seen as blatant racism, properly ostracised and even possibly illegal. Here, where nearly half the population was black, Sambo and Mammy held equal sway with Che.

'Hard to understand,' said Alex, rifling through a display of beer-can coolers and drink coasters featuring drunkenly unconscious black men with crosses for eyes.

'Only two dollars,' said the dark-skinned stallholder.

That evening, tiring of the standard of free food at the Internacional, they chose to stay in town and pay for dinner. However, they found the meal choices limited and the waiters distracted by a local baseball game on TV. It seemed that restaurant staff everywhere preferred to watch the game rather than serve meals. One restaurant eventually relented and took them in. But as the couple deliberated over their food selections, their heavily sighing waiter said sarcastically, 'Why don't you take the menu home?'

They ate their *ropa vieja* quickly and left. They were waiting for a cab back to the hotel when they were accosted by two giant golliwogs.

'Good god!' Alex muttered. A skipping Sambo and a waddling Mammy, as wacky and single-minded as football club mascots, huge heads rolling on their shoulders, were making their way along the street, stopping traffic, posing for photographs and shaking hands with passers-by.

As Sambo, arms outstretched for an embrace, bore down on her, a flustered and embarrassed Amanda cried out, 'Oh no, I just knew it! Alex, do we give them money?'

'I don't know.' He was nervously getting out his wallet. But as the big-buttocked Mammy sashayed up to him, agitating her booty, she shook her massive head, and from the depths of the head a deep male voice said calmly, 'No need,' and then Mammy hugged Alex to her padded body.

*

Back at the Internacional the nightly after-dinner entertainment was about to begin. A local dance troupe was setting up on the terrace, facing the sea. The wind had scarcely relented since morning and a flapping canvas sign declared, in English, *Rhythm of the Night.* Partly visible behind the sign, three girls and three boys were changing into glittery dance costumes. The girls smoked cigarettes as they dressed.

Alex and Amanda easily found a table. They ordered free mojitos and sat back in the sea-wind to watch the performance. The wind scraped a plastic chair over the edge of the terrace and tumbled it a few metres along the sand.

Amanda shivered and pulled her cardigan tighter. 'What on earth are we doing?'

'Soaking up atmosphere,' Alex said.

'Very funny.'

'Look over there,' he said. On the far edge of the terrace sat the mankini man and the Cuban boy.

'At the same table!' she said.

The man was dressed in a long-sleeved white shirt and trousers and the wind was blowing out his shirt tails and ruffling his wispy hair. The boy was smoking, his eyes on the dancers' preparations, and his face was more animated than usual.

'He's dressed up for a night out,' Amanda said. 'And they're actually sitting together. It's a proper date. Finally. I'm glad.'

'You old romantic,' Alex said.

In chipped heels and laddered tights, the troupe came out from behind the canvas sign to dance. The wind howled in from the ocean, the girls' hair blew across their faces, but in the difficult conditions, on the sandy and slippery terrazzo slabs, moving to recorded music, they prevailed.

More than that. They succeeded. No dancer faltered. They looked proud, glamorous, professional and poised. They seemed optimistic that somewhere in this audience of rum-drunk Russians and beery Canadians was an international impresario eager to dress them in un-laddered costumes and immaculate shoes and sign them up for bigger engagements than the mouldy, Batista-era Hotel Internacional in Varadero, Cuba.

They performed three routines. And anticipated their cue for the next. The young *Rhythm of the Night* dancers stood frozen in dramatic pose as they waited for the music to resume. And waited. Their music-player sat on a bench, suddenly unmanned. Where was the music for their next routine? Where was their DJ-choreographer? Had he or she fled the weather, the discomfort, the company's existence?

Still the dancers stood waiting, immobile, still proud, but stopped in their tracks, willing the situation to be different. Gradually they began sneaking glances at each other and putting their hands on their hips, and slumping. Embarrassed for them, the audience started to sigh and mutter. More time passed.

To Amanda and Alex, years, decades, it seemed. Still no music. No more rhythm this night.

Mortified, the lead dancer, a handsome brown-skinned youth with a shaved head, gave a furious grunt and they all strode off together to the shelter of their windblown canvas sign, shoes clicking on the terrazzo slabs, heads held high.

The small audience clapped wholeheartedly. The sympathies of several nations went out to the dancers as they gathered behind the sign, muttering, cursing, wandering in tight angry circles, consoling each other and lighting cigarettes. As they began changing out of their costumes, the Cuban boy left the mankini man at the table and joined them. Alex and Amanda saw him commiserating with the lead male dancer.

'Uh-oh, here's trouble,' Alex said.

The young men hugged like old friends, and when he saw them talking animatedly, arms still around each other's waist, and then casually kiss, the mankini man rose abruptly from the table and walked down to the beach.

Only a few minutes passed before the Cuban boy glanced back to the table and noticed the man's absence. The boy left his friend and the grumbling dancers, and in the light from the terrace he followed the mankini man along the windblown sand to the shoreline, calling his name.

So the man whose beach costume and melancholy nature had so amused and intrigued the travellers had a name. To Alex and Amanda, the boy seemed to be calling *Walter!* Then the thin man and the boy following him both walked beyond the terrace light and out of the couple's sight and thoughts and their vacation narrative.

As it happened, melancholy Walter walked purposefully into the ocean, further than thigh-deep this time, and was immediately swept up in a rip. The Cuban boy, whose name Alex and Amanda had not discovered, followed his bobbing blonded head and billowing white shirt into the surf and tried to rescue him.

Walter was carried three hundred metres north along the Hicacos Peninsula and dumped, exhausted, on the shore amongst some beached and broken paddleboats. The Cuban boy, who could barely swim, was swept away and drowned.

The next day, Alex and Amanda Emerson would return on the bus to the beguiling atmosphere of Havana, to experience the haunts and habits of José Martí, Ernest Hemingway and Graham Greene. As with the ubiquitous Che, there was no getting away from José and Papa. Back to the Ambos Mundos, the Hotel Sevilla, El Floridita, Finca Vigía.

However, this windy night at the Internacional in Varadero they left the terrace for the warmer saloon inside, ordered a last free mojito and optimistically tried to check their emails. But there was no wi-fi, as advertised. The hotel computer was 'not working yet'. This news didn't surprise them.

Lavender Bay Noir

One humid Sunday morning in February when the scent of frangipanis hung heavily in the air, Brian Tasker stood in his yard overlooking Lavender Bay while his mother-in-law shaved his body.

Sunlight glanced off the surrounding oleanders and frangipanis and flickered through the native fig trees clinging to the cliff behind the house. The cliff marked the boundary of Luna Park, the harbourside funfair, and between the loops and slopes of the dormant roller-coaster that came to rumbling, screaming life every sunset, a mirage quivered on the surface of the bay.

While Dulcie Kroger was kneeling and spreading shaving cream over her son-in-law's legs, he tried to concentrate on the way the mirage lapped like a windswept lake on the boatshed roofs across the water. But once she began wielding the razor, working upwards from his size-thirteen feet, up his shins and calves to his thighs, he found it difficult to maintain interest in an illusion.

During dinner the evening before, he'd mentioned something Alf told him at training. 'Guess what?' he said to Judy and her mother as he dug into the five courses Dulcie had served him,

'The Yanks have had a bright idea – shaving their bodies before a race.'

'Seriously, Brian?' wondered Judy, her eyes twinkling. After six months marriage he still found her wide-eyed look and little-girl giggle intriguing and adorable. She knew it, too, which made her even more provocative to him. 'Shaved all over?'

A delicate creature to look at. Her chirpy laugh, blonde bob, bright nails and arms like twigs belied her nervous intensity. Full of nervous energy, a fast walker, someone who ran up and down stairs, a chatterer, she seemed hardly to eat.

Compared to his meal – tonight it was chicken soup and buttered bread, six lamb chops and vegetables, potato salad, sliced bananas and ice cream, and cheese and biscuits, washed down with two glasses of milk – hers was miniscule: one chop, a smidgen of mashed potato and a smattering of peas to push around her plate.

'*All* over?' her mother repeated.

'The whole body,' said Brian. 'All the exposed bits, anyway. They reckon it makes them swim faster.'

Alf Wilmott, his longtime coach, had picked up this intelligence from an American friend who'd observed a training session of the swimming squad at the University of Southern California.

'Shaving-down eliminates drag,' Alf told Brian as he dried off after his afternoon hundred laps of the North Sydney municipal pool. He'd been his coach ever since Junior Dolphins, where he'd recognised the talent of the skinny nine-year-old who'd been brought along to swimming classes to help his asthma.

More than a coach, really. A mentor, almost a father figure. Then through all the high-school and district victories over his teenage years, and the regionals, and his successes at state level. And now, if all went to plan, to the nationals and the selection trials for the Australian team.

'We'll give it a shot,' Alf said. 'The psychological effect makes you swim quicker. They say you feel smooth and slippery like a fish. Transformed.'

Brian didn't need reminding he needed to swim faster. To be transformed. As Alf repeated, unnecessarily, the Melbourne Olympics were only nine months away, in November. The Australian team would be selected in August, after the national titles. And there was another Sydney swimmer, Murray Rose, dogging his heels. Rose's times for the 400 and 1500 metres freestyle almost matched his. And they were improving, and he was still only sixteen.

This boy Rose was a handsome *wunderkind,* a blond prodigy who defied swimming's traditions. For a start he was thin, rather than conventionally barrel-chested and broad-shouldered. And he trained in Sydney Harbour. *The harbour? With its tides and waves and oil spills and flotsam.* Moreover – veteran sports writers shook their heads in wonder – the kid was a vegetarian.

They struggled to recall any top athlete who'd been vegetarian. Who didn't exist on steak. The papers set up photographs of wet-headed, muddy-footed young Murray standing on the harbour foreshore after training, towel looped around his neck, skinny ribs poking out, happily munching a carrot or a stick of celery.

Such a novelty. The newspapers were happy to provide the on-camera veggies.

Brian knew Melbourne was his last possibility to make an Olympic team. His BSA Gold Star motorbike, slippery tram tracks on the Lane Cove line, and a broken elbow had ruined his chances for Helsinki in '52. So he sold it. No more physical risks. He'd be twenty-four by the time of the Games in November; and twenty-eight, positively elderly, by the next Olympics, in 1960.

'Get out the razor this weekend,' Alf said. 'We'll do a time trial on Monday.'

*

Brian thought he'd surprise Judy with his new smooth body when she came home from St Francis Xavier on Sunday. Surely anyone could put a new Gillette in their razor and shave themselves down? But standing there in the sunny yard in his skimpy racing costume, cursing with the effort, he found it surprisingly tricky. How to shave the backs of your thighs? How to avoid nicking the tender skin behind your knees? The grunts, the near-naked contortions: a neighbour or passer-by might have wondered what was going on behind the frangipanis and oleanders.

Dulcie was watching this comedy through the kitchen window and she came out into the yard. She was wearing a swimsuit, too: pale blue and strapless, in some sort of elasticised satiny material.

'Come here, furry boy,' she said, and took the razor from his hand.

It was like a mild electric shock at first. As she scraped the razor up his shin and thigh to the edge of his swimsuit, his focus on the wavy roof mirages of Lavender Bay was fading fast.

'Relax, kiddo,' Dulcie said. 'I used to be a nurse.'

This was evident in her proficiency: in her frowning attention to her task and the frequent pauses to rinse the razor to keep the blade keen.

As if experience, her knowing boldness, changed anything. While Dulcie continued shaving his thighs Brian stared across the bay and tried to fight the reaction of his body and mind. A feeling somewhere between excitement and fear, stimulation and embarrassment. This woman kneeling before him, strands of auburn hair brushing his skin, her tanned cleavage looming below his eyes, was his mother-in-law!

After she'd finished his thighs, she rose to her feet, rubbed more shaving cream on his stomach, and as a tremor ran down his body she performed a professional depilatory operation on the furry track of his abdominal hair.

By now Brian was blinking rapidly and finding it difficult to regulate his breathing.

'I've seen it all before,' she went on. 'The male body's nothing new. I've done this a thousand times.'

That made him feel even younger. In her competent hands he felt naive and innocent, a self-conscious adolescent. His heart was still hammering when she rinsed the razor again and attacked the curly hairs on his chest. As she worked, she hummed a sentimental song from the hit parade. 'Oh! My Papa'.

In a greater effort to distance his mind and body from Dulcie's matter-of-fact razor work, Brian lifted his gaze to the sky where a pelican hovered over the bay, higher than he imagined possible for such an ungainly-looking bird. Then as his mother-in-law glided the blade carefully over his pectorals, gently circumnavigating the nipples, the pelican became a tiny soaring white blotch.

The sun beat down. '"Oh! My Papa",' Dulcie hummed. In the native fig trees on the cliff, a clumsy flock of black cockatoos rustled and fed. The pelican skimmed out of sight.

Brian closed his eyes on the sky. Orchestrated shapes like dew droplets or oil globules floated in patterns behind his eyelids and he could feel the sun's rays on his upturned face.

Now Dulcie stood on tiptoe. 'Head up, Tiger,' she said, and in four strokes she swept the razor from collarbone to chin. 'Right arm up,' she ordered. Brian's arm hung tentatively in the air, trembling slightly. She had to steady it to shave his armpit.

'Now the left one.' Unhindered now by hair, a trickle of suds ran down his chest and stomach. Eyes still firmly shut, he heard the cockatoos continuing to squawk and eat, and half-gnawed figs plopping on the ground, and a train clattering across the Harbour Bridge towards the city.

By now the breeze felt overly intimate on his exposed skin. His body was disconcertingly sensitive – electrified – and the female smell of her olive skin and her satiny swimsuit made him light-headed, giddy with his intimate proximity to a semi-naked, mature woman on a summer's day.

Dulcie took up his right wrist again, held it steady, and swept the razor up his forearm to his elbow, then along the triceps to the shoulder. She paused there and put her free hand on his right shoulder and clasped it for a few seconds, and closed her eyes as if considering its muscles and tendons and reflecting on the exercise that had gone into its formation. The hundreds of miles it had swum.

Time stopped. Then she shaved the other arm, and for a moment she closed her eyes and squeezed this shoulder, too.

'All done, Johnny Weissmuller.' She dropped the razor in the pot of water and ran both hands over his chest. 'Smooth as a baby's bottom.'

*

When her second husband and Judy's stepfather, Chief Petty Officer Eric Kroger, shipped out for nine months on the destroyer HMAS *Warramunga* a month before, Dulcie had moved in with her daughter and son-in-law. The Australian navy, the *Warramunga* and, by extension, CPO Kroger, were assisting the British in maintaining the security of the Federation of Malaya against Communist insurgents.

The arrangement suited both households. Dulcie had company while Eric was away, and though Brian was doubtful at first, the young couple found they benefited from her help around the house, and especially with his Olympic preparation.

Soon after their marriage, Brian and Judy had been delighted to find the house for rent above Luna Park. A two-bedroomed nineteenth-century shipbuilder's cottage, its sandstone walls and narrow back garden bordered by oleanders and frangipanis, it suited the newlyweds' romantic mood. Importantly, it was only a hundred yards from Alf Wilmott's coaching headquarters at the North Sydney pool, and only two train stations across the harbour from Judy's night-shift copytaker's job at the *Daily Telegraph*.

Brian, meanwhile, was working as a phys. ed. teacher at North Sydney Boys High, a welcome job for an amateur athlete. The pay was only Education Department standard rate but the school was just a mile from their house, easy jogging distance, he had use of the gym, and the hours suited his early-morning and afternoon training sessions.

Unlike most new husbands, Brian soon welcomed his mother-in-law's presence. This was because of her cooking and his huge fuel requirements. Five miles twice a day in the pool, plus his weight training, burned up mountains of calories. And, frankly, Dulcie was a superior cook to his 21-year-old wife.

In any case, Judy's new night-time job absented her at dinnertime during the week, so Dulcie's cooking was crucial. Only at weekends did Brian and Judy get to eat meals together. Or, for that matter, go to bed at the same time.

Their clashing schedules was the only impediment to marriage harmony. While Brian rose at four-thirty for his five a.m. laps, and was asleep by eight-thirty at night, Judy's shift on the *Telegraph* ran from four p.m. to midnight, the newspaper's busiest hours. When Brian arrived home from school she was off to work, and he had to immediately leave for the pool. And after catching the last night train home from Town Hall station, Judy fell exhausted into bed – her head ringing with domestic crimes and gang stabbings and gambling-den raids – around one a.m.

From Monday to Friday, Dulcie prepared Brian's evening meal. After dinner, in deference to her excellent cooking, her role as Judy's mother and her status as an elder relative (she was forty-four), he'd chat politely with her over a cup of cocoa. Then as his eyelids began to droop, he'd stretch his weary limbs, say goodnight, climb the stairs and hit the sack.

*

On Sunday mornings Judy hurried home from Mass so the young couple could make up for their love drought during the week. As Sunday was his only break from four-thirty rising, Brian was excused from church, allowed to linger in bed, catch up on sleep, and wake refreshed for her return to bed at eleven.

On this particular rest day when she returned home from church, Judy was puzzled to find Brian wasn't in bed as usual but sitting in his bathrobe in the backyard. He was drinking coffee and reading the *Sunday Telegraph*. Recalling the shaving-down conversation of the night before, she peeled back his bathrobe.

A transformation. His hairless chest looked strangely pale and vulnerable. His back was striated with scratches. Shamefaced, he said, 'My first try at shaving myself.'

'Idiot. I would've done that for you.' She stroked his wounded shoulderblades. 'Poor baby.'

In the kitchen her mother was making a clatter with pots and crockery and impatiently switching radio stations back and forth from a haranguing evangelist on the Worldwide Church of God to a country and western couple yodelling competitively. The radio was hopeless on Sunday mornings.

'What's up with her?' Judy murmured. She picked a pink frangipani blossom and put it behind her ear. 'Back to bed, smooth fish,' she whispered.

As he trudged upstairs behind his frisky adorable wife, she continued to scold him. 'Fancy trying to shave your own back. You don't grow any fur there, thank goodness.'

*

It wasn't only the lazy mornings that Brian relished on Sundays. At around one-thirty the couple would rise languidly, put on their swimsuits, and head to Bondi Beach. This afternoon Dulcie was keen to join them.

After his hundreds of pool laps during the week, it was a luxury for Brian to swim purely for pleasure, to catch waves, to enjoy the ocean. Today the salt water made his shaved limbs tingle and stung his back in an unfamiliar but sensual way. Indeed, after a surf, a milkshake, a meat pie and a hamburger, sunbaking on the sand with Judy and Dulcie stretched out on either side of him, Brian felt sated, as pampered as a sultan.

Judy's hand openly stroked his newly sensitive left thigh. And as Dulcie turned on her back and adjusted her swimsuit to expose a fraction more chest to the sun, her knee or foot surreptitiously brushed his smooth right calf.

The sea, the warm rays and the tasty takeaways were such great revivers of a young athlete's body and spirits that the sultan was soon speculating on the week ahead, suddenly a bewilderingly different and arousing vision, beginning with this evening when he and this slender blonde girl presently wriggling against him would be in bed again.

When this did occur several hours later, however, a loud knock on the bedroom door interrupted them. Judy groaned. How long had Dulcie been standing there, within earshot?

'What's the matter, Mother?' Judy called out. 'We were fast asleep!' Clearly false, but difficult for an eavesdropper to contradict.

'I've brought you some cocoa.'

'We don't need cocoa!'

'Brian always has a cup of cocoa at this time. It's part of his training diet.'

'God! Leave the cups outside the door then.'

'I can't. I'll spill them.'

Brian's back was smarting. He was suddenly exhausted.

Judy rose, strode naked across the room and opened the door. The women faced each other. Neither was smiling. Judy took the cups of cocoa.

'Thank you,' she muttered.

'Put something on,' her mother said.

Judy shut the door on her and returned to bed. Brian's eyelids were drooping as the couple lay waiting for Dulcie's footsteps to go downstairs. In the long silence Judy thought she could hear her mother breathing outside the door. Eventually the stairs creaked and shortly afterwards plates and cutlery were rattling and cupboard doors banged in the kitchen.

'Where were we?' Judy whispered to Brian. He was nearly asleep but he rallied valiantly to the cause.

*

On Monday afternoon when Alf Wilmott put his 1500 metres specialist through a time trial, the newly shaved-down Brian Tasker swam the distance 3.5 seconds slower than in his natural hirsute state the month before.

'Heavy weekend, boyo?' Alf asked, shaking his head. 'What happened to your back?'

Brian shrugged. 'Shaving-down,' he said.

As punishment, Alf made him swim an extra three miles, made up of ten 400-metre swims within an hour, with an average time of four minutes forty-five seconds, representing about ninety per cent effort.

*

There was no reason for Brian to shave down the following Sunday; the whole point was to shave just before a big race, so your body felt the difference – the transformation – and reacted accordingly. But as soon as Judy left for church, Brian was in the garden with the shaving cream and razor.

Under low humid clouds the day headed sullenly towards a thunderstorm. Cicadas buzzed a monotone refrain in the trees. A mirage juddered across the bay. While he waited, Brian watched the tiny Lavender Bay ferry steaming across the harbour and the illusion was of two mysteriously conjoined boats, the regular ferry and, above it, another misty ferry that churned boldly over the water's surface and through the air. For some reason he thought of his nemesis, the up-and-coming young harbour swimmer Murray Rose.

Soon Dulcie joined him. She'd changed into her blue satiny swimsuit and heat radiated off her flesh. With a frown, she examined him. Only a shadowy stubble showed on his limbs and chest but she lathered his body and began shaving him anyway.

The westerly breeze from the harbour was warm and humid and carried smoke from a bushfire in the Blue Mountains. But Brian shivered. The air was pungent with the smell of burning eucalypts and the drone of the cicadas was deafening. As the two twinned Lavender Bay ferries approached Circular Quay, they slowed, then docked, and their images merged back into a single small boat.

'I need to be thorough,' Dulcie said. When she finished, she ran her fingertips slowly over his body. Neither of them had spoken until that moment. As she drew him into the house and upstairs, he asked, 'Have you trimmed your fingernails?'

Her glistening eyes aroused and unnerved him. She didn't answer.

*

There was an abrupt change in Brian's weekday routine. Now when he got home from his afternoon pool laps, damp-headed and smelling of chlorine, Dulcie was waiting by the door to take him directly upstairs to her bed. Afterwards, she served him his customary big dinner and bedtime cocoa.

One time only, feeling more ravenous than usual after training, Brian suggested dinner before bed. But the instant they'd had sex he fell deeply asleep. It was difficult for Dulcie to wake him.

'Come on!' she urged him. He'd fallen into a noisy dream, thrashing and breathing heavily, as if he was swimming in his sleep. Maybe he was racing in the Olympics and took her urging for a cheer squad's encouragement, for he began to flail even more and breathe faster and faster.

'Ross!' His arms and feet were striking her. The bed was about to collapse. The floor as well. It was after midnight and she started to panic. 'Oh, Ross, wake up!'

'Ross?' Brian mumbled. Ross Gooch had been Dulcie's first husband. A rugby front-rower for Randwick, big Ross had died in bed of a heart attack at thirty-one.

'Judy's dad,' said Dulcie, the word 'Judy' rousing him enough for her to coax his body out of her bed, across the landing, and into his own.

*

From then on, Dulcie insisted on bed before dinner only. As for Sundays now, Judy was slightly mystified that Brian waited in the shade of the frangipanis and oleanders for her return from church. And that he'd always shaved himself again – even attempted to shave his back. They headed upstairs of course, but Brian seemed wearier these days.

'Poor boy, has Alf increased your training load?'

He shrugged. 'We've had to step it up. The Games are getting closer.'

Her heart went out to him: her champion. Usually he thrived on tough training, and he'd worked so hard for this. Ever since he was seventeen and she was fifteen, high school sweethearts, he'd had this grand ambition: the Olympics. As the Games drew closer it was understandable he was feeling stressed.

He'd even lost interest in their Sunday morning pillow talk. After they'd celebrated her return from Mass – although not as playfully and energetically as they used to – Brian just wanted to go back to sleep, whereas in the past they'd lie there chatting about the past week's newspaper gossip.

As a copytaker, she was well up on the news. As deadlines drew closer, reporters out on the road would phone in their stories to the copytakers. Sitting there in her headphones, typing up the paragraphs they dictated from the nearest public phone, she'd get the news from the courts, police beats and crime scenes even before the editors did.

A recent juicy story she'd planned to discuss with Brian was a case of thallium poisoning on the North Shore. On discovering her husband Keith's numerous extramarital affairs, Thelma Teasdale, in the *Telegraph*'s words 'a respectable Roseville housewife and a regular finalist in the Royal Easter Show's cake-baking competition', had put rat poison in his breakfast cup of tea.

As the paper's science reporter, Warren Baxter, a lugubrious fellow known in the newsroom as the Undertaker, wrote in a rider to the Teasdale murder trial, 'Known to the police as "inheritance powder", "wives' revenge" and "the poisoner's poison", one gram of odourless and tasteless thallium sulphate in cakes or scones, or mixed in hot drinks, can slowly and subtly kill an unsuspecting victim.'

The Undertaker added helpfully: '*Thall-Rat*, the brand favoured by Thelma Teasdale for poisoning her husband, is freely sold in hardware stores nationwide.'

Thelma Teasdale's crime was only discovered because her husband's brother Raymond was a chemist. Keith's dizziness, stomach pain and nausea were at first put down to New Year's overindulgence. But when followed by pains in the hands and feet, agonising leg cramps and total hair loss, Raymond looked up his old pharmacology books. When Keith died at only forty-two, Raymond declined Thelma's offer of tea and cake at the wake and went to the police.

Just the sort of juicy crime news Brian usually enjoyed. But he showed no interest in the Thelma Teasdale story so Judy didn't pursue it.

However, when she arrived home from her next shift she definitely called his attention to another news story, waking him with tearful ferocity at one a.m. Bursting into the bedroom, she smacked a first-edition *Telegraph* on the bed and pushed the offending page, smelling of fresh ink and still warm from the presses, into his sleepy face.

The copytakers' room was envious enough of Judy's marriage to a handsome swimming champion for an older unmarried colleague, Thelma Jackson, to hasten to point out the story to her. 'Look at these bitches cuddling up to your hubby!' Thelma frowned sympathetically, adjusting her glasses to better perceive the girls' guile. 'Mind you, he doesn't look too upset about it.'

The photograph in the sports pages showed three grinning female swimmers, slippery as seals in their wet racing costumes, stroking Brian's muscular bare chest and shoulders. Brian was flexing his right biceps and beaming back at them. An accompanying caption said:

> Super-smooth Olympic 1500-metres hopeful Brian Tasker proves popular with the girls as he displays his new shaved-down physique at North Sydney Pool.
>
> Coach Alf Wilmott is recommending this innovative American trend for his entire male swim squad. 'For extra speed, even a fraction of a second, my boys will be shaving down before big events,' Wilmott says. And long-distance specialist Tasker looks enthusiastic. 'I'll try anything to give me an edge,' he says.
>
> The girls (from left), backstroker Rowena Flynn, 18; breaststroker Maxine Vanderhaag, 19; and up-and-coming freestyler Carole Sinnott, 17; certainly endorse Brian's sleek new look!

Dazed and defensive, Brian sat up in bed. 'It was a posed picture, a set-up by the photographer,' he protested. He didn't recognise Judy's fierce tortured face, the bared teeth and projectile tears.

'Just a bit of fun. Some girls in the squad fooling about for the camera.'

'You're a married man,' she sobbed. 'I suppose you're sleeping with them all?'

It was his turn to be indignant. 'Don't be ridiculous!'

She ran out of the room, crying, 'I never want to see this disgusting sort of thing again,' and left for the couch downstairs.

*

When Brian returned from his early-morning training at seven, Judy was sitting with Dulcie at the kitchen table with the offending sports page in front of them. Both women were smoking cigarettes and drinking tea, and they fell silent and glowered at him as he entered.

'You're up early, love,' he ventured to Judy. He was exhausted from exercise, sleeplessness and emotion.

She drew on her cigarette, said nothing, and stared at him with tragic possum eyes.

'*Popular with the girls,*' Dulcie quoted. She gave the newspaper a disdainful backhand slap. Her eyes were glistening. 'Surely you can't expect your poor wife to be able to sleep after that?'

*

That afternoon at training the swim squad passed around the paper, laughing and teasing each other about smooth Brian and his 'fans', and the girls all complaining, ridiculously, that they looked fat in the photo. Shortly after, Brian's next 1500 time trial did not go well. He'd lost another 6.08 seconds.

Alf frowned and looked anxious. 'What's the matter, son?' he wanted to know. 'You look buggered. Everything all right at home?'

'Sure.'

'Well, take ten minutes rest, you bloody slowcoach, then I want another 800 at ninety per cent effort.' And Alf stamped off.

Dusk was falling and little commuter ferries steamed back and forth across Lavender Bay. Above the pool, dozens of nesting swallows flitted about the stands and skimmed over the water's surface. To one side of the pool, trains rumbled home over the Harbour Bridge; on the other, the eyes, teeth and lips of Old King Cole, the giant grinning face at the entrance to Luna Park, suddenly lit up, startling the swallows perched on King Cole's eyelashes.

At twilight the Art Deco cornices of the stands and change rooms, built when the North Sydney Pool had proudly hosted the 1938 British Empire Games events, seemed more gloomily ornamental to the swim squad than they did to their sleepy eyes at dawn training.

Ever since Alf had moved his team from the Drummoyne pool to North Sydney's superior facilities two years before, Brian had been a little in awe of this place, the venue for an extraordinary eighty-six world-record-breaking swims. As he recovered his breath, his eyes followed a flight of swallows to their nests above the topmost stands.

Sitting in the back row was Dulcie, staring down at him.

*

When he arrived home an hour later, she met him at the door. Oddly, for this hour, and the cool evening temperature, and being indoors, she was wearing her satiny blue strapless swimsuit.

She pulled him towards the stairs. She'd applied fresh make-up and her body was shiny with perfumed lotion.

He noticed her eyes had that eerie gleam. 'I don't think so,' he said. 'Not any more. Why were you spying on me?'

'In order to check on you with your young girlfriends, you cruel bastard. You'd better come with me so I can punish you.'

He was speechless. Her urgent tugging released the now familiar warm scent of womanly flesh, and the satiny fabric of the blue swimsuit brushed against his face with its own erotic smell, and his anger, bewilderment and weakened resolve had no resistance. Afterwards, because of her wild fingernails, his back was scratched even more painfully than usual.

*

When Dulcie greeted him at the door the next evening, he managed to avoid her embrace. He found it alarming that she was wearing her swimsuit again.

'I saw you watching me at the pool again,' he said. 'I can't do this any more. Seriously, it has to end now.'

She smiled coquettishly. 'I have to make sure Johnny Weissmuller is behaving.'

'Everything is peculiar about this,' he said. 'Being shadowed by my mother-in-law is very weird behaviour. I'm twenty-three. I've got a marriage to think of, not to mention the Olympics.'

'I'm too old for you now, is that it? And I'm weird!' She began to weep. 'You lead me on, and now you prefer your teenage sluts.'

He groaned. 'They're not. I don't. Jesus Christ, I'm calling a halt for the good of everyone.'

Dulcie wiped her eyes and sighed theatrically. 'Sure you are, you monster. Come and sit down for your dinner then.'

She spun on her heel and he watched her swimsuited thighs sway towards the kitchen. In the doorway she turned abruptly and kissed him hard, and pressed her body against him, and he followed her upstairs once more. Afterwards, she said to him, smugly, 'I bet those girls aren't as good at this as I am.'

Speechless, he just shook his head. His shoulderblades had left spots of blood on the sheets.

*

Brian and Judy walked hand in hand through Old King Cole's monstrous mouth at the entrance of Luna Park. Sydney's traditional weekend entertainment spot was so close to home yet this was their first visit since moving to Lavender Bay.

It was Brian's idea. So was leaving the house quietly, without involving Dulcie. 'We need some time alone,' he said.

They strolled along the boardwalk, past the merry-go-round, the Spider and Dodgem City. They rode the Wild Mouse and bought milkshakes and chips and fairy floss. The roller-coaster rumbled overhead and the night was punctuated by customers' screams. A breeze from the bay ruffled Judy's skirt and blew ice-cream wrappers across their path.

Outside Dodgem City four young sailors were chatting to three older women. The sailors were egging each other on with nudges and winks, and smoking flashily, with tough-guy hand gestures. They looked no more than seventeen and wore their caps so jauntily far back on their heads, behind waves of pomaded hair, that the caps seemed to defy gravity.

'Come on, girls,' one of the sailors said. The women looked bored. Sparks flew over the dodgem cars and the air smelled of electricity.

Brian felt Judy's grip tighten and her shoulders stiffen as she urged him away.

'What ride would you like now?' he asked her. 'The Big Dipper? The Ghost Train?'

She shook her head. 'Did you see those girls?'

'The ones with the sailors? Yes, why?'

'What did you think of them?'

'Prostitutes maybe.'

'Attractive? Your type?'

'Hardly! What's this about?'

'I'm trying to work out what sort of women you go for.'

'*Your* sort. Jesus, Judy!'

Her smile was tight and her eyes seemed shiny and unfamiliar. 'Come home then, and show me how much that is.'

As they walked back through Old King Cole's mouth, two incoming teenage girls, heavily made-up and tottering on high heels, elbowed each other and giggled. The bolder one called out, 'Hey, aren't you Brian Tasker?'

He nodded in polite acknowledgement, but Judy glowered at them. Her mood worsened when she heard the girl mutter, 'What's up with that titless bitch?'

'Lucky slut,' said the other one.

At home, Dulcie was sitting in the dark garden. She looked pale and jumpy and her hair was awry, as if she'd been pacing in the wind. She was underdressed for the night temperature and she had a frangipani flower stuck behind her ear.

'There you are!' she said, over-brightly. 'The two lovebirds!' She raised her voice over the rumble and screams of the roller-coaster. 'I'm having a sherry. Will you join me?'

'Not in the mood, thanks Mum,' said Judy. 'We're off to bed.'

*

When Judy returned from Mass next morning, Brian was sitting in his bathrobe in the garden again, sipping a cup of cocoa and staring sleepily across the bay.

She pulled open his robe. 'So you've shaved down again!' she said, and slowly shook her head.

'I need to be transformed,' he said. He reached a languid hand out for his cup but misjudged the distance and his hand fell short. 'Sit down and have some cocoa.'

Dulcie was watching from the kitchen window. 'There's no more cocoa, Judy,' she said firmly.

'Don't worry. I'll make a pot of coffee,' Judy said. 'Brian looks as if needs a coffee.'

Brian gazed around the garden. 'Yes, I'd like a coffee now. Everything's a bit blurry this morning.'

Judy said, 'I've been worried about your cuts and scratches. Sitting out here among the oleanders. They're so poisonous, you know.'

*

It was during his next 1500 metres time trial on Monday that Brian Tasker collapsed at the 1350 metres turn and became tangled in the lane ropes.

Still holding his stopwatch, Alf Wilmott, Brian's coach since Junior Dolphins, jumped fully clothed into the pool, disentangled him from the ropes, and held his head above water. But by the time Brian was hauled from the water, laid on the pool deck and resuscitation was attempted, he was dead.

At the inquest the city coroner found that, tragically, repeated severe exertion had further damaged the clearly genetically-defective heart of an otherwise gifted athlete.

His grieving widow attracted wide public sympathy after the *Telegraph*'s pictorial coverage of the funeral service at St Francis Xavier, attended by top sportspeople from a wide range of activities, including the up-and-coming swimming star Murray Rose.

Two years later, Judy Tasker, still only twenty-three, married the *Telegraph*'s young police reporter, Steve McNamara. By this time, after winning three gold medals at the 1956 Melbourne Games at the age of seventeen, Murray Rose was a national hero.

In April 1958 when CPO Eric Kroger and the *Warramunga* left for six months' exercises with the Far East Strategic Reserve, it was convenient for all concerned for Dulcie Kroger to move in with her daughter and her new husband.

A View of Mt Warning

Russell Garrett and Mike Hodder had been friends ever since primary school. They'd made speeches at one another's twenty-first birthday parties and as best man at each other's weddings, Russell doing the honours at both Mike's weddings, the big Anglican ceremony at St. Mark's and the marriage celebrant's more relaxed affair held at low tide between Tibetan prayer flags on the sands of Cape Byron.

Now, over New Year's Day pre-lunch beers, while the meat sizzled on the barbecue and Mike's second wife Sophie prepared the salad indoors, Russell winced at the knowledge that this year they'd both turn fifty. So they'd known each other forty-five years. 'Food for thought, eh?' he said, as he allowed the shiraz to breathe.

Their youthful bond had been tight, never more so than one icy August morning when Mike dragged the heavier Russell, concussed by a tourist's errant surfboard, first to the surface and then ashore. And of course Russell's occasional physical backup to Mike's teenage braggadocio. Other than those forty-five years, however, Russell and Mike had little in common nowadays.

Now they were friends simply because they'd always been friends. They'd stayed in touch despite their lives taking different paths, maybe *because* their lives had taken different paths. And because they lived nine hundred kilometres apart and only saw each other three or four times annually, including every New Year at the Hodders' house.

Since their North Coast surfing adolescence Mike Hodder had dropped out of engineering at UNSW, married his high-school girlfriend, leapt into Northern Rivers real estate, made a pile in the sea-change boom of the nineties, divorced and remarried, and retired early to Byron Bay, to a three-story Wategos Beach cliff-house, a vertical engineering feat poised dramatically above the humpback whales' migration route.

Over recent visits Russell had perceived a gradual change in his friend. The wit and imagination Mike had shown in snapping up both the striking Sophie Howson and that prized white-water view – of the same exposed point break and north-east swells they'd surfed endlessly at sixteen – were no longer evident.

Drastically, in Russell's mind (he still kept his old boards ready for action in the Hodders' garage), Mike seemed to have wearied of surfing. In his premature retirement, having attained the woman and house he wanted, Mike appeared to be letting life pass him by. He was taking it easy. Comfortably and purposefully ageing, he spent his days in his shuttered study, forgoing the vista, the beach, the health-giving ocean, for his wine cellar and cable television's endless spool of sports.

Russell Garrett, on the other hand, living and working far from the ocean, was running the same old race year after year. He'd emerged from veterinary science at Queensland Uni to take over an old-established horse practice at Rock Forest, outside Bathurst in the central west. Eschewing sick cats, dogs and canaries for horses meant worse hours and considerable travel and inconvenience (horses had a habit of falling ill on public holidays), and he couldn't afford to retire. Garrett Equine Services had seen both ends of thousands of those surprisingly frail, nervy and accident-prone creatures, with no doubt hundreds more extremities to come, and lately Russell's life was the most exhausting it had ever been. His marriage had broken up twelve months before, at the start of the equine flu epidemic. It had been a rough year for a country vet.

So while the atmosphere at the home of his longtime friend was initially more awkward without Estelle present, and with Mike oddly engrossed in TV sports round-ups, Russell's first two beers of the year didn't touch the sides. New Year's Eve had been taxing, unexpected and, finally, sleepless. But January 1 was supposed to be a day of optimism. Although slightly rusty in the joints, he'd already hit the beach and the early-morning swells curling past the cape. The surf had worked its old magic and he was on holidays in familiar company on the coast he loved. The dead year was over and done with, and now lunch was fragrantly grilling on the barbecue.

Reclining in a deckchair on the Hodders' terrace, Russell was surrendering to the sunny breeze and the sweeping panorama of the bay and the Nightcap Range. For the first time ever he was searching for another conversational opening when Mike, lowering his voice as he flipped the steaks, murmured, 'I had enough of those bloody spam emails pestering me. So I gave Viagra a whirl.'

'Really?' Russell felt his left eyelid twitch. When it kept fluttering he turned his attention to the view. As always, his eyes sought out the tallest peak, rising through the mauve clouds today like a holy Shangri-la mountain. Mt Warning, named by Captain Cook as he sailed north on the *Endeavour* in 1770, and steeped in Aboriginal spirituality for many millennia before that. How many school projects had he prepared on Mt Warning? How many mountain ranges had he built out of egg cartons?

His eyelid still fluttered involuntarily. Understandably in the circumstances, his nerves could still take him by surprise. For at least ten years – in fact, ever since the day of their marriage – he'd been enraptured by his oldest friend's wife.

'Well, it definitely works,' said Mike. 'What with that and the coke, I was like a bloody eighteen-year-old again. I felt like I was in a porn movie.'

At no level did Russell want to hear this. He could bear the idea of Sophie and Mike Hodder's physical relationship only if it was conducted as he observed it: vertical and fully clothed. His was a melancholy and insurmountable jealousy, compounded by guilt. Of course his feelings for Sophie were unrequited, but even if she'd been aware of them and magically, enthusiastically reciprocated, she was the wife of his boyhood friend – Mike's second and sixteen-years-younger wife – and therefore out of bounds, now and forever.

Such was the nature of his infatuation, however, that even as he tussled with guilt one moment, deliberately avoiding her presence, the next minute he'd be torturing himself with the smallest hints and snatched glances. She'd bustle and bend and flip her hair from her forehead and he'd have to tear his eyes from the thrilling sight of her rinsing dishes at the kitchen sink, arranging flowers, making coffee. This woman's actions were never mundane.

It was obvious she liked talking to him, and often seemed to sparkle in his company. She must have noticed that at any party, after several drinks, he self-consciously drifted to her side. Indeed, she often blithely joined him, too. Sometimes she even flirted with him, and his blood pounded with the excitement of possibilities. But then she'd cheerily turn elsewhere, and behave the same way with Mike's other friends, and he'd feel like a sulking fifteen-year-old. Sophie was a friendly person.

In saner moments back in the Bathurst district, bouncing along a gravel road on his way to deal with some Shetland's or Arab's hoof-thrush or rain scald, or an old thoroughbred's well-earned arthritis, he reasoned that her public squeeze of his arm, the chest prod or cheek pat, was merely her tactile nature. Or was she subtly testing him? Was Sophie a tease? No, she was a decent, straightforward person. But at night before sleep he was at his least realistic. How could he not dwell on the *perhaps* and the *maybe* and the delicious *what if?* As he had last night, of all nights.

Whenever he saw her she had him in a flurry of confusion. In her presence, aching for her trailing hostessy fingers, the accidentally brushed knees, the casual touch, he always felt like a teenager. As she passed by his chair he'd clench his stomach muscles and surreptitiously flex his biceps. Willing her, *touch me.* Then he felt like a fool.

As time passed and Russell tossed these conflicting day-dreams back and forth after every get-together, he still managed to keep his feelings hidden. He was doomed to silently adore everything about her, from her generous spirit and quick humour to that slight overbite and mole on her upper lip. Of course he noticed these small flaws; every imperfection was a sensual asset.

It wasn't just physical attraction, he convinced himself. He genuinely admired her. While he envied her loyalty to her husband, he also respected it; the way she dutifully waited on Mike with drinks and food. Sophie *attended* to him. The thing was, he, Russell, also *liked* her – and of course phlegmatic Hodder, entrenched in front of Fox Sports all day watching lacrosse and snooker and Japanese rugby, a mid-morning jug of bloody marys by his elbow, a sequence of afternoon and evening wine bottles, didn't deserve or appreciate her at all.

When Russell thought about it, not since the moment he fell for her, at their windy wedding on the Cape, with the northerly whipping the Tibetan prayer flags and exposing the laughing bride's thighs, had he seen Mike embrace her. Or even touch her. On Sophie's behalf, Russell was offended. And gladdened.

It was bewildering how Mike could treat her so neglectfully when he, Russell, was so overwhelmed by her creamy limbs and cleavage and careless dark hair – the whole sexual package – that he fell into a brief catatonic state whenever they hugged hello and goodbye.

While he dwelt regularly on the look and feel of Sophie, recalling the lively pressure of her body in those jolly public embraces, as time passed after each contact he'd momentarily come to his senses. He'd be standing in some urinous country stable or faecal paddock, shin-deep in mud and cow pats, crows gagging overhead and the whiff of something decomposing nearby, and he'd say it aloud: 'It's a dream.'

It would never come to anything. In his marriage to Estelle there was a bond, and three grown children, and a long rapport he wasn't willing to deny. Stamping back to the Land Cruiser, full of sad determination, he'd once again place the possibility of a romance with Sophie in fantasy territory, in the bittersweet category of never-to-be. A sweetly carnal version of winning lotto.

Then, quite abruptly, these overlapping quandaries produced some new dilemmas to both confuse him and rekindle his hopes. The first, a surprise to him, if not to Estelle, was that their marriage of twenty-four years suddenly disintegrated. Nothing to do with his longing for a fantasy woman whom he'd never even kissed. One summer afternoon she left.

It was Estelle who pulled the plug on him, and Dan and Nick and Lily, in order to embark on the 'personal journey' she'd apparently promised herself before she turned fifty, and as soon as the children reached twenty-one. She also made it clear that her journey was not a trip that stopped at his station.

Maritally jettisoned, he would have been more devastated if it hadn't been for the equine epidemic. Oddly, the horse flu got him through; he was so overworked he didn't have the time to languish. And eventually, as the disease finally ebbed, it dawned on him that he was single again, no longer required to be a dutiful and faithful husband – maybe there was a bright side to this – and in the usual dark three a.m. cave of despair there appeared a chink of light. He'd soon be seeing Sophie again.

Now on this first day of the New Year, as the piquant smoke of beef marinade drifted across the terrace and out to sea, here was Mike waving barbecue tongs and slyly muttering, 'I did my Viagra research up at the Gold Coast. At good old Madame Peaches.' Almost simultaneously, two electric flashes struck Russell. *So, not with Sophie.* And then, *Mike visits prostitutes.*

Russell made the appropriate responses, the whistle, the raised eyebrow, but his beer suddenly tasted metallic: flat, warm, like sucking cutlery, and he poured himself a shiraz. My God, Mike was winking at him. Mike was grinning. Mike did a little disco jig so his chest jiggled in his T-shirt, and he snapped the barbecue tongs over his head as if they were crab nippers or castanets. His oldest friend had turned into a sleazy, alcoholic shithead.

He kept his voice flat. 'You go there often? To brothels?' Five or six times a year, he gathered. Mike and three cronies disappeared on rollicking all-boys sporting holidays to Brisbane, Sydney,

Melbourne, the Gold Coast. To Test matches, football finals, race meetings, fishing trips – and brothels. Much avid organising was involved. The Veterans' Sporting Club, they called themselves. The VSC.

'You're now in the company of the president of the VSC,' Mike announced. He'd come to life all of a sudden. The sunlight brought out his new high colour, the pouchy eyes and broken veins. Russell thought he saw a hint of jaundice in Mike's eyes, but they wouldn't meet his. Mike snippety-snapped the meat tongs again and attempted more weak humour.

'Order, order! The meeting will come to order!' This rare garrulous outburst was like being earbashed by a drunken stranger in a pub.

At this point Russell recognised something of powerful and limitless potential. Also something that would never occur. Despite its possible rewards – their marriage instantly ending and Sophie flying into his sympathetic arms – the idea of him spilling the beans, or even indirectly allowing the beans to be spilt, was beyond the pale. The Old Mates Rule. Mike knew that. It went without saying. And if he did do so, Sophie would despise the messenger. And he'd despise himself.

Russell hated Mike at that moment. Even with a mouthful of wine, he still tasted knives and forks on his tongue.

Mike gave the barbecue a moment's attention, put down the tongs and yelled out to Sophie, 'Steak's ready!' Then to Russell, he said. 'Thanks again for last night, by the way. Missing the party and all.'

Russell sucked in some sea air. 'No trouble.' Much of New Year's Eve had passed in a reeking stall in the stable of Mike's hinterland property at Clunes. Not that he regretted it. Here Sophie Hodder kept her four horses – three geldings and a 22-year-old bay mare. In the late afternoon the mare had lain down, writhing and kicking and snapping at the dirt, and refused to stand. No local vets were available on this major party evening and Sophie had phoned him in tears. The horse was in a bad way. It was seven o'clock by then, and he was still an hour south on the Pacific Highway. He hadn't even begun his holiday. 'I'll meet you there,' he'd said.

She was wide-eyed and agitated when he arrived. Western-clad, kneeling by the horizontal mare, jumping up, pacing and waving her arms, she came across like a feisty rancher's daughter in a cowboy movie. He was always deliberately calm and calming on the job, to animals and to people. He patted her shoulder. 'I remember seeing you try out this old girl,' he said.

Seven or eight years ago he'd been there at her request to check out the mare's condition; she was thinking of buying her. He'd watched them walking the riding arena, the clearest memory. The metronomic gait of the horse, and Sophie's body flowing into the rising trot. Black hair swinging below her helmet, strands gathered in a child's ponytail. The jounce of her breasts increasing in the canter; the rise and fall of her tightly jodphured seat. The hypnotic sexual tempo of her ups and downs.

'So, should I buy her?' she'd asked him.

He even recalled the pale-blue polo shirt, her exercise-blush from cheek to neck, and the frown of concentration that completed her intensely female look. Her vividness made him feel countrified and khaki-coloured by comparison. He could have eaten her up, boots and all.

'You look good together,' he'd said.

Mike had remained in the car throughout, reading the sports pages like a bored father.

This time she was in grass-stained jeans, from kneeling. 'Help me get her on her feet,' he said. 'Let's walk her.' In the fig trees around the paddock, squealing fruit bats were rousing themselves and flapping heavily over their heads. The patient had colic.

'Horses are drama queens,' he said.

By ten-thirty he'd led the mare into the stable stall and with mineral oil and a stomach tube induced her to defecate freely, whereupon she snorted, stamped, tossed her head, and soon recovered. He was still holding the mare's head-collar and both of them were shit-soiled when Sophie leaned in and kissed him. She had straw in her hair. Just a quick kiss of gratitude, but firmly on the lips.

In those first hours of the New Year, even after the long drive to Wategos and several drinks, Russell found it hard to sleep. All along the coast, snatches of laughter and party music carried on the breeze.

Eventually the voices and music faded, and doors slammed, and cars drove away. Once, his body jumped to footsteps on the stairs. At first light he would get his old malibu from the garage and hit the water. But until dawn he lay alert, listening to the mixed rhythm of the surf and Mike's proprietorial snores rumbling from the master bedroom.

*

The Hodders served a simple New Year's lunch on the terrace. Steak, Moroccan salad, local fruits – tamarillos, guavas, papayas, mangoes – and cheeses to suit the wines. Summery Australia stretched ahead like a double-page spread in a travel magazine. The south-easterly tempered the heat of the sun, and in the small waves off the Cape schools of surfers and dolphins gently surged and mingled. Like the Paramount Pictures trademark, or the volcano it had once been, Mt Warning rose dramatically from the lavender clouds over the range.

Positioned on the edge of the terrace so he wouldn't miss a ball or a single run, Mike's widescreen TV displayed the murmuring green vista of a cricket match. Russell wondered if Mike was using the cricket to avoid conversation. This was ridiculous. After lunch he said to his old surf companion, 'The wind's changed. Get your board. They're pumping.'

'Maybe later,' said Mike.

By mid-afternoon the breeze had dropped altogether and Russell and Sophie strolled down to the beach for a swim. Mike declined in favour of the cricket and a chilled bottle of pinot grigio.

And so passed the first day of the new year. As night fell, Mike was dozing in his study in front of a Korea-Estonia soccer match. Their swimming costumes long since dried on their bodies,

Russell and Sophie were drinking on the terrace and in no hurry to end the evening.

To avoid the moths and Christmas beetles, Sophie turned off the terrace lights and they sat in the dark. To Russell, in a rare daze of fatigue, confidence and good humour, this was surprisingly thrilling, reminiscent of childhood Murder in the Dark and Spin the Bottle. In this pleasant state he discovered that without any conscious effort they were sitting confidentially together, their knees and foreheads almost brushing.

Somehow their bare knees soon did connect, and remained firmly pressed together. The warmth this created seemed important and correct for such a pair of rapidly conjoining souls. Neither their intent expressions nor their conversation changed when he put his hands on Sophie's cool upper arms and squeezed them for a few seconds. Though the smallest alarm bell sounded with the touch of her smooth biceps, it was stilled by a blood-tingling new sensation, like the continuation of an actual dream: a glorious lack of restraint.

Below them the tide sparkled like soda. 'I'm allowed to be drunk,' Russell said, looking down at the beach. 'Firstly, I'm on holidays. Secondly, I'm not driving. And thirdly, I'm watching stingrays hunting in the moonlight.'

It was true. In the moonlit shallows, working gracefully in unison, a school of rays was rounding up silver pilchards. The rays were ushering the tiny swarming fish into shore, enveloping and cornering them, and in their skittering panic the pilchards trailed strings of phosphorescence.

As much about the change in circumstances as the glistening hunt below, he asked Sophie, 'Is this happening, or am I imagining it?'

'Something's happening,' she said.

Their foreheads lightly touched. Although it may have been melodramatic and dated of him to ask so solemnly, 'Can we kiss now?', after ten years of infatuation and frustration it seemed chivalrous and fitting. So he did, and there was no hesitation from Sophie. Still sitting, bare knees pressing against bare knees, they held each other and kissed for a long moment.

The sensation of kissing her seemed so unique that new words were needed for the open moist warmth of her mouth, her lips' softness, the willingness of her embrace. When they eventually drew apart, it was with shock at themselves and the world's sudden echoing silence.

The television was off in the study and the stillness was abruptly broken by the clattering rumble of the refrigerator's ice server. It thundered like an avalanche. Ice cubes tumbled endlessly into what must have been the world's deepest glass. Finally the rumbling stopped. The door from the terrace to the kitchen was open and Mike was standing by the refrigerator, wearing only purple boxer shorts in a dice pattern and staring out into the dark.

*

Russell lay in the spare bedroom recalling the rapture of the kiss on the terrace – he still couldn't believe it had actually happened – and the shock of being caught out. His pulse pounding in his ears, he relived the kiss over and over again. He felt both marvellously elated, and nauseous with disloyalty. What had happened to his principles?

But had the kiss really been spotted? Mike hadn't said anything. Perhaps the timing had just favoured them by a second or two. It had probably been too dark anyway. Did Mike see them, and then purposely make that din with the ice cubes? Or, dulled by booze and sleep, had he blearily padded into the kitchen, filled his glass with ice, then randomly gazed out to sea?

Fortunately they'd been too stunned to panic. In any case, it would have been crazy to jump up guiltily from the embrace. Hopeful of that one or two extra seconds, they'd remained where they were, slanting marginally away from each other now, giving the impression of being a couple merely engrossed in conversation. To a witness it would clearly appear to be a serious tete-a-tete, maybe over-familiar, but less intimate than being caught kissing the host's wife.

Russell could almost convince himself there was nothing to worry about. Mike had stood there, his stomach overlapping the dice-patterned boxers, filled a glass with ice, uttered nothing, and exited the room. So after a short interval, as if at a given signal, he and Sophie emphatically scraped back their chairs, moved around busily, chatting loudly while clearing plates and carrying glasses to the kitchen sink.

They stood at the sink, rinsing their wine glasses and looking obliquely at each other. He saw Sophie's cheeks blooming with the same flush as the day she had cantered her new mare in the arena, the day he had felt sixteen again, hollowed out by excitement and tension, and perilously in love.

Wily as a spy, he glanced around and stepped forward to risk another kiss. She raised her eyebrows at his nerve, patted at his chest and kissed him again.

Shortly afterwards, calling 'Goodnight, goodnight!' they went upstairs to their separate bedrooms and he lay on top of his bedspread, still in his board shorts, his head swimming.

The next sound to register was a kookaburra at dawn, and when he struggled to the toilet, headachy and half-asleep, the reflection of the sun was a golden radiance filling the bathroom mirror. Immediately he remembered the kiss and its aftermath, and was both euphoric and anxious all over again.

It surprised him to see he was still wearing his board shorts from the day before. Convenient, though; he needed to hit the surf immediately to clear his head and provide a breathing space for the events to follow. Time to think things out.

But her kiss still filled his mind. From the bathroom window the sky was red over the Cape and strings of parrot-coloured cloud streamed across the horizon. A sullen swell was rolling ashore and the dawn seemed charged with pre-storm electricity. The thought of her lying just metres away, warm and sleeping, and the incontrovertible fact of their liaison, made him catch his breath.

On his way downstairs he heard the TV going in Mike's study. The sound made him even edgier. But sooner or later he had to face him. He forced himself to look into the room. Mike was slumped in his armchair, a succession of neck, chest and belly rolls flowing down his torso, a kimono hanging open over his boxer shorts, sipping a bloody mary.

'Morning, Mike,' Russell said. Was it his guilt that put him on the front foot now, made him sound so disapproving? 'Six o'clock. You've put the boat out early.'

'Good morning. And it's only juice.' Mike's hairless, bone-white legs were up on the coffee table. Yesterday's cricket highlights flashed past on-screen, each highlight – a six over the fence, a shattered wicket, a difficult catch – greeted by a mysteriously loud crowd reaction from spectators' stands that appeared almost empty. Mike drained the glass and looked up. His red, puffy eyes could be blamed on excessive alcohol. Or, the thought abruptly shocked Russell, on recent weeping.

'I suppose a surf is out of the question? Do us both good,' Russell said.

'Not today.'

Russell felt so uneasy he had to ask. 'Are you okay, man?'

'Hunky-dory, old fruit.' Still half-gazing at the TV, Mike reached into a kimono pocket and withdrew a small packet. 'Industrial strength, recommended by this Chinese quack up the coast. I've been looking forward to trying them out. I took two, they should be working pretty well by the time she wakes up.' He made the universal fist and stiff forearm.

Russell's eyelid began vigorously fluttering.

'Trouble is, when they dilate your blood vessels they make your eyes bloody red.'

Russell's eye-flutter proceeded apace.

Mike turned towards him now. 'I've got the Veuve in the ice bucket. I usually do some smoked salmon. Caviar. Hard-boiled egg. Little toasty fingers. I go to a bit of trouble for our extravaganzas. Sophie likes a long decadent breakfast beforehand.'

Russell began heading out the door. A tin-coloured sea loomed all around and the mountains were indiscernible in the clouds.

Mike called after him, raising his voice over the television. 'Listen, could you do us a favour and stay out there in the water for a couple of hours?'

The SeaDream Emails

Hello! I finally managed to grab a computer after waiting for Linda from Adelaide to take a toilet break from tracing ancient relatives on Ancestry.com and boring Brad from Brisbane to check his share portfolio!

Unlike me, the other passengers are experienced cruisers and know all the lurks – like hogging the wi-fi at every opportunity. (Our phones don't work at sea – I don't know why.) I'll try to email you my news whenever I manage to snatch one of the two computers in the Horizon Lounge.

Maybe it's the group effect aboard ship or perhaps people are happy to find a stranger of a certain age to talk to, but everyone unloads their life stories on you in the Club Bar. When they see you're a woman travelling alone it just pours out of them.

Fortunately, they're not interested in hearing anything from a sixtyish school teacher on her long-service leave from Rosemount High – and on her first-ever cruise. That suits me! There's an upside to the invisible years! They just want to talk about themselves and boast about all the other cruises they've been on. 'Oh, is this only your first? This time last year we did the Adriatic.'

I must say I was surprised at the number of old-timers and invalids boarding the *SeaDream* in Costa Rica. Walking sticks and wheelchairs. Snowy-headed men with big ears and wrinkles. Bent old ladies. Leathery old geezers limping from strokes. All day they play bridge and check the stock market and look up dead family.

How was Costa Rica? Apart from hot, very pretty in a hilly tropical way. In our twenty-four hours in San Jose we visited a waterfall and a mountain and an eco-zoo of butterflies and jaguars and a couple of ocelots. All just smallish cats lying in the sun and not at all menacing. The jaguars were particularly disappointing. I expected something at least slightly savage looking. Then we were ushered into a cage where hundreds of butterflies alighted on me. Strangely off-putting, I must say.

The Costa Rican tour guide, a huge woman in khaki, called the toilet 'the happy place'. Well, after a couple of hours of bottled water and the local coffee there were a lot of people lined up waiting to be happy, I can tell you. Vultures soared above us at all times. From our ages they must've thought they were on to something.

*

Here are some fellow passengers I've met so far. The couples start with Leon, a Dutch ex-stockbroker, and his wife Dawn. He's got Parkinson's and was interned by the Japanese in Java during the war. Then there's Charles and Yuko, a Melbourne lawyer and his Japanese wife. And Runo and Karen, a wealthy-looking Estonian businessman and a New Age American woman from Taos with long plaits and Indian jewellery. She's a vegan iridologist, you'll be surprised to hear. They meet once a year for a month's cruise together, than go back to their normal lives of being complete opposites.

And there's Joan and John, a talkative, tapestry-crafts, mannish sort of woman and her ex-teacher husband from Wollongong. He sits up very straight like the teacher's pet in school. 'John's got Alzheimer's,' Joan announces in front of him when they meet new people. This is awkward. John's always dressed like a primary-school boy in short-sleeved shirt and short, elastic-waisted pants pulled up high, short grey socks and sneakers. I made some friendly, fellow-teacher-type remarks to him but he just stared straight ahead and pulled up his socks.

The Singles next. There's Olaf, a lovelorn Swedish businessman and widower who's trying to woo Jane, a retired doctor. Linda the ancestry buff. And Doug Monk, a talkative former pharmacist who's full of facts on everything, like ships' tonnages and speeds and the names of seabirds. He's a keen birder. ('Frigate bird at two o'clock,' he says. God save us!)

And the computer hogger, Brad, a noisy Brisbane businessman who buys a garish comical T-shirt in every port and then wears it to dinner. He has a head of carefully tended, suspiciously dark hair in the early Beatle style, like an eighties current-affairs host. He goes hatless in the tropical sun. When I asked him, 'Aren't you going to wear a hat, Brad?' he answered loudly, for everyone's benefit (the other men are mostly bald), 'No point, I've got hair.' Brad loves his hair.

Did I tell you I've been handing out little toy koalas and kangaroos to the locals in each town? To shopgirls and waiters and such. 'For your children,' I tell them. After forty years, I miss the kids, I must say. Some ex-teachers don't at all, but I do.

My koala distribution made Doug grab my wrist in San Jose and say to me, 'Has anyone told you, Beverley, that you have a very warm nature?' I think he's trying to crack on to me. Only the wrist so far, thank goodness!

*

There's another older woman on board, Susan (who I call the *SeaDream* Socialist), travelling with a much younger husband, Cliff. She told me she was enthralled with Mao, Fidel, Ho and others in her youth, and travelled to China in the 1970s. One afternoon she escaped from her group in Peking and headed down an alley with a friend where they came across an old man doing beautiful calligraphy in a room with a guard.

He spoke English, so they conversed pleasantly for some time. Later Susan rejoined the group and told their tour leader. He said, all excited, 'You stumbled on to the last Emperor of China!' Well, the younger brother actually, who was heir to the throne.

Susan said she recently read that he was still alive today, living in Beijing, still under guard and spending his days doing calligraphy. For some reason, she didn't want me to repeat this story. 'Keep this to yourself,' she said. And here I am telling you!

What I found interesting about this idealistic old socialist, who seemingly once had a successful career in the public service (and who encouraged her partner to turn down an ambassador's job because she wasn't interested in the responsibilities of an ambassador's wife as it would curtail her own travel plans), was her final comment:

'Oh, I love *SeaDream* cruises.'

Why? I asked her.

'Because of the butler service – they look after you so well.'

*

Of course all the birders on board flocked to last night's lecture, 'Birds of Central America', with Dr Raoul Martinez, a Colombian naturalist. Tonight it's 'Marine Mammal ID', with Dr Raoul again, the next night a screened doco, *A Man, A Place, A Canal.* Doug Monk, the party's keenest birder, crossed swords with Dr Raoul over the global distribution of the blue heron.

It got a bit heated, with Dr Raoul suggesting that Doug was confusing it with the grey heron, and maybe even the white heron, which got Doug riled ('I know my herons!'), and to escape the heron ruckus everyone fled to the Club Bar.

Over drinks there I overheard the oldest gang talking about 'Green Dreams'. Dr Jane (unmarried, tall, good dresser, great colour coordination) later volunteered the news that Cath, Dennis and Roy were planning to check out pharmacies at the ports en route for those euthanasia pills freely available in Belize and Panama and Mexico and throughout Central America.

When I sat down they'd been boldly discussing the Green Dreams. Jane said they meant Nembutal, the death pill. Roy was also announcing defiantly that he's 'ninety and going strong', and Dennis said proudly he was 'a young eighty-eight everywhere but the knees'. Cath didn't say, but she's probably mid-eighties. They seem pretty fit and happy to me so maybe the Green Dreams are just a precaution for the bedside drawer.

Jane had already volunteered that she's in cancer recovery herself and that 'No one gets to see me naked these days'. From the ardent look of him, Olaf wants to try though!

There's one 'younger' couple on board, Bevan and Jessica, probably early fifties, with the look of second-marriage newlyweds, maybe on their honeymoon. Anyway they're rattling the cages of some of the older couples with their affectionate public displays.

Not the men so much, but definitely the older women. 'I'm glad Leon and I aren't joined at the hip,' one older woman (Dawn) bitched. The honeymooning woman is especially demonstrative. I bet they're the only passengers having sex.

The only passengers maybe. But the word in the Club Bar is that the tour controller, Hannah Jansen, a vivacious thirty-something South African, is having an affair with the captain, Sigge Nilsson. He's Swedish, tall, blond and only about forty. When glances and murmured instructions pass between them there are winks and nudges all around.

*

I must tell you about one more passenger – Ingrid. She needs an email on her own. In the Sydney departure lounge I'd spotted this skinny, gaudily dressed old bird sinking champagnes and already loud and tipsy. As we belted up for the flight to Mexico she plonked down next to me so I said, 'Good evening.'

Her response was a curt 'I guess so'. OK, I thought, what a rude one you are. After a couple of hours in the air, impatient with the staff's resistance to serve her more wine, she asked me to press my attendant button for drinks – for her. While we waited, a string of complaints followed about the flight ('a Mickey Mouse airline') and just about everything else.

She came from Melbourne ('Bleak City', she called it), and when I inquired if she was travelling alone, she said, 'Of course. I won't travel with my husband any more. He's just a bloody nuisance since he's had his guts cut out.'

People were preparing to sleep, but Ingrid complained that she didn't want to yet. When the wine supplies cut out she sighed loudly, grumbled, stood up, took off her red jeans and bra (I'm not joking!), everything but her knickers, stood bare-breasted in the aisle and changed into her airline pyjamas.

The flight attendants rushed over. 'You can't do that here, madam!' But Ingrid insisted. 'I get claustrophobia in those stupid toilets.' What were they going to do? Throw an old woman off the plane at 35,000 feet? Next morning she stood in the aisle again, shed her pyjamas, bared her boobs (very perky, obvious inserts, I kid you not), and got dressed again.

As luck would have it, Ingrid was joining the *SeaDream* cruise too. It turned out she was a loner. She discourages company, hangs around by herself smoking like a chimney, and is always the first into the Club Bar and the last to leave.

Every night, Diego, the on-board entertainer, plays romantic ballads on his keyboard. He reads the lyrics on a computer screen.

He sings in English but I don't know if he understands what he's reading. His Filipino version of 'The Lady is a Tramp' goes, 'She don't play crap games with barons and eels'. *Eels!*

Every night Ingrid gets up by herself and dances. Diego claps her and gives her the thumbs up as she swings her bony booty like she's eighteen!

Guess what she announced to all and sundry in the Club Bar on our first night at sea? 'I'm not getting involved with anyone on this trip. No more rumpy-pumpy for this girl. I'm seventy-eight and I'm closing shop.'

Diego launched into his syrupy interpretation of 'Satisfaction' and Ingrid began prancing about like Mick Jagger. We all looked at each other, and people raised their eyebrows and stared into their drinks. At this stage no one was used to Ingrid yet.

*

I must tell you about our stopover in Honduras. We're at the Las Palmas resort for the day. Intermittent rainstorms as we shelter under cabanas. The beach is man-made – sheets of plastic laid over the reef, with sand dumped on top of them. The seabed is shallow, but slippery and oozy to walk on. And Leon with Parkinson's is wading out by himself. He's two hundred metres out, but in only about two feet of water, not much more than knee deep, when he slips over and can't get up. He's struggling and going under, constantly slipping and falling face first.

I'm the only one in the tour party to take notice. His wife Dawn is drinking mojitos in a cabana and not watching him. Nor is anyone from the ship, or the tour organisers. So I run into the water and wade out to him, pull him up – he's face down and thrashing and spluttering – and with difficulty get him to his feet.

He's a heavy chap, Leon. And I support him and walk him into shore. He's in a state, panting and snot streaming, and can't talk.

At this point the tour doctor, Graeme Fitzsimmons, behaves strangely. He photographs us stepping onto the sand but he doesn't move to check Leon at all. The whole tour staff's attitude is peculiar. Though no one has actually voiced that he was in danger, they're instantly denying it. 'He's fine,' Hannah Jansen says loudly. 'Looking good, Leon!' They've turned his close call around. Terrified of bad publicity, I'm guessing. And a legal suit.

'Silly of him to swim by himself,' they murmur. 'But we were onto the situation from the beginning.'

Leon might easily have drowned but no one thanks me for lifting him up and bringing him into shore. Strangely, neither Leon nor his wife speak to me either after that.

*

Guess what? Ingrid disappeared in Panama City yesterday. She wandered off from our shore party in the Old Quarter. Panama's not the sort of place to go missing. We walked up and down the lanes looking for her, peering into stalls run by Indians with faces and costumes out of history. No Ingrid.

Our bus waited and waited in the heat. Sailing time was getting closer, our crew was panicking and eventually they called the tourist police. Finally Ingrid was escorted aboard by the cops. Turns out she'd gone looking for a bar, got caught up with a mob of Spaniards and eventually joined their group from another cruise ship.

Early next morning we're all out on the top deck watching in our bathrobes as we enter the locks of the Panama Canal. Fascinating to watch, as the *SeaDream* creeps along, only millimetres separating the ship's sides from the locks' edges. Two determined egrets follow the ship all the way through the canal. Surely, I think, there can't be any fish in the constantly rising and falling and violently churning water.

'That's typical egret behaviour,' says Doug Monk.

Ingrid's on deck, too, smoking, in a red silk robe, but she's deliberately not looking at the ship's progress through the locks. She's going through the once-in-a-lifetime experience of the Panama Canal while deliberately turning away from the activity! She's a strange one!

I forgot to mention that she's in my muster station for lifeboat drill. So is Doug Monk. As we stood there in our lifejackets listening to the drill announcement, Ingrid was rolling her eyes in boredom and ostentatiously smoking beside a *No Smoking* sign.

Doug whispered something to me. 'Beverley, If we're shipwrecked and starving and floating in this lifeboat for weeks in the middle of the ocean, I want you to know I'm not eating Ingrid!'

*

Last night the oldie gang all got animated in the Club Bar about that young Australian couple who jumped overboard last month from the *Islander Princess*. Remember? It was all over the media. Very sad business.

I can easily visualise the hour before the incident. Drinks. Old jealousies. An argument at dinner. A break-up is threatened. The girl gets emotional. Wanting to make a dramatic gesture, I'm guessing, she climbs over the railing, stands there a long moment on the ledge, waiting for him to say something that will change things. It had better be good. A few seconds of silence pass, or maybe he's desperately pleading. For an instant she holds complete power.

And then she jumps. Immediately, her boyfriend jumps after her. His natural instinct. So it's curtains for him, too.

He was a country-town paramedic, Roy said, and it was in his gallant nature to save people.

The terrible tragedy that can result from a moment of madness! All night I couldn't stop thinking about them struggling in the ocean. Next day when I prised a computer away from Brad, I googled *Cruise Passengers Overboard.* Well, you'd be amazed how often it happens. Guess how many people go overboard and drown in the sea? On a luxury cruise? On their holiday of a lifetime?

An average of twenty-four people a year have gone overboard in the last five years. Two people a month. The average age of a passenger who jumps overboard is forty-one and you're most likely to go overboard (either fall or jump) on the last night of your cruise. For some reason, people from California and Florida go overboard more than others.

The good news. Well, good-ish. Falling overboard doesn't always mean you'll drown. Sixteen people have been rescued since

2000 – one a year – one woman after eighteen hours in the water. Not great odds though: one in twenty-four saved.

Naturally most people who go overboard are drunk or doing silly things, showing off by climbing on the railing or between cabin balconies. Males mostly. No surprises there.

*

You know that genteel dining-room routine aboard passenger ships where the captain and the ship's officers spread themselves around at dinner? Each table gets an officer. Of course the captain's table is the prime spot. My table got the ship's doctor.

But Dr Jaime and I struck up an interesting conversation. Turns out he's on his first cruise, too. He's early fifties, I estimate. He said he's winding down professionally. His first job was emergency surgery in Mexico City but his most recent position was with a company that sold a cancer treatment taken from the venom of the blue scorpion.

The blue scorpion is found only in Cuba. They electrocute the scorpion (but don't kill it because it's too too valuable) to make it release the venom. This is mixed with water, then used to destroy tumours.

The only problem, according to Dr Jaime, is there aren't enough blue scorpions to meet the demand. Their reproduction in captivity is very difficult. Even though each female scorpion gives birth to about forty-five young, they easily die in the laboratory.

The venom is extracted by a mild electric shock to the scorpion. This extraction method causes considerable damage to the scorpion over time, so they're only kept for a limited period, and then set free into their natural environment to breed.

Not surprisingly, the Cubans don't have a licence to sell this alternative medicine into the US or Europe, with the exception of Albania. So you have to get your stock of blue scorpion venom from Albania.

Scorpions? Albania? I queried if it actually worked, and he said his mother had a tumour on her face that cleared up after the blue scorpion treatment. He nearly lost me when he said cheerfully he'd take it himself, if necessary, 'Because I want to grow to a ripe old age like you.' The cheek!

At the end of dinner, however, after more wines, he gripped me by the elbow as I was leaving the dining room. His eyes went all puppyish and he said, 'Success rate is about forty per cent, the same as most serious pharmaceuticals. But not enough for me to spend my life on blue scorpions.'

I spent most of today on the top deck. Ingrid was sitting by herself there, smoking, while hundreds of flying fish sped above the ocean. I said, 'Morning,' as always, 'Aren't they great?' indicating the flying fish glistening in the sun, and she grunted, as always, and turned away.

An elderly Swiss fellow on the deck agreed with me about the flying fish though. I hadn't met him before – Klaus, a retired accountant. He told me he flies to Cuba every six months for a week of salsa dancing. Don't you love the idea of a Swiss accountant loosening up on the dance floor in Havana?

*

Sorry for the email drought, I've been out of action with the stomach bug that's hit the passengers pretty hard. I didn't leave the cabin – or the bathroom – for three days! Every second person has the gastro. (The others all have bad colds!)

When you mention the sickness that's hit everyone, the tour staff all change the subject. The tour doctor, Fitzsimmons, is the worst. 'Just rest,' he says. 'Keep taking liquids. You look okay. You must have picked up something ashore.' Poor Dr Jaime is running ragged, looking after everyone. The tour officials are all in denial. But suddenly there are signs on the door handles advising you to wipe your hands on the antiseptic pads provided.

I forced myself out of my cabin to take a convalescing canoe ride up a jungle river in Guatemala. Or was it Colombia? I was pretty groggy and hollow by then. Anyway I thought I saw a two-toed sloth in a tree, then two more, one with a baby. And spider and howler monkeys. And a basilisk or 'Jesus Christ' lizard (yes, their real names). So many blue herons that even Doug lost interest in them. And turkey vultures. I get a funny feeling whenever I see vultures. Doug discounts them too.

I pulled out of the tour of the banana factory though. Coming from Queensland, I can't get excited about bananas.

*

That canoe ride must have been in Guatemala after all because yesterday we anchored near a shanty port called Livingston where the local Garifuna people were selling *I Love Guatemala* T-shirts. Ghostly-looking boats were moored there, many half sunk, covered with pelican guano and smelling fishy. Pelicans the same colour as their guano squatted on every inch of space on the wrecked and deserted boats.

Doug and his fellow birders aren't over-thrilled by pelicans and egrets either. However, he did emphasise several times that unlike your normal Central American egret ('also known as the white heron'), these birds couldn't wade because there was no available ground to wade on. They had to perch on trees because the overgrown jungle cliffs here reach right down into the river. There wasn't even room for mangroves to grow. In the surrounding trees, more monkeys swung from branches.

Doug said he preferred the birdlife of Belize, our latest port of call. Apparently Belize is noted for its varied and colourful birdlife, especially the red-footed booby. Doug bought a T-shirt announcing that he's now a member of the Belize Audubon Society, founded in 1969. It has a red-footed booby on it.

I'm feeling much better today. It's been a beautiful day on Half Moon Caye, off the Belize mainland. Doug and I went for a walk along a deserted jungle path during which he informed me that this sandy island supports four thousand breeding birds, 'the only viable red-footed booby breeding colony in the western Caribbean'.

'Amazing,' I said. Then he made a pass. My first one in thirty years. You know, like riding a bike, it comes back to you.

Even in the sand!

This news goes no further!

*

Today, our second day in Belize has been totally different – the hottest day yet of our tour. Belize City is said to be built on a foundation of logwood, mahogany chips and old rum bottles. The port was jammed with tourist boats from the US. Young men dressed as pirates greeted the arriving cruise ships and huge Americans on three-day tours from Florida waddled along the wharf.

In the afternoon Doug and I played truant from sightseeing in the heat and passed up the House of Culture, the cathedral and the former jail-turned-museum and found a breezy bar on the harbour where Doug ordered icy cold Belikin beers and a DJ played Bob Marley and old pop songs, and drink waitresses in tight clothes bopped to the music. I felt about twenty again. Well, forty-five.

From the bar we saw the ageing members of the *SeaDream* party returning exhausted and sweating from their tour of historic buildings. Ingrid was at the rear of the group, sauntering along alone. Smoking, of course. We saw her entering a pharmacy that advertised, in big type on its window,

Special Price Drugs for Tourists!
Everything You EVER Need!
Viagra! Valium! Nembutal!

Doug and I looked at each other. 'Good god!' he said. 'Green Dreams!'

'At the end of her tether,' I said. I felt guilty for not trying harder to befriend her. Surely I could have done something.

Ingrid came out of the pharmacy with a small package and entered the bar. She strolled to the far end of the room, and as she walked up to Diego the Club Bar musician, sitting at a table in the corner with two cocktails waiting, she wiggled her hips, *ka-voom,* and they kissed.

Spotting Killer Whales

On Sunday afternoon my brother and I were sitting at the window table at The Shelter, a smart new restaurant in Yallingup overlooking the ocean, when I saw something break the surface just outside the surf line and I said, 'There's a killer whale!'

Mack looked out to sea and frowned back and forth. The ocean was murky and seabirds skidded over the low waves. A grey swell was slapping right on shore and no surfers were bothering with it. In the weed and cloud shadows it was easy to imagine things.

'It can't be,' he said. 'There are no killer whales this far north. They like cold seas. It must be a humpback or a dolphin. Or a shark.'

He pointed to the sign on the beach cautioning fishermen against cleaning their catch on the shore. The sign said this could attract sharks to the swimming beach.

'Now they're a protected species there's always a great white or two hanging about out there,' Mack said.

Mack's an adamant person. He grumbles that sentimental conservationists now regard the great white shark as 'the new dolphin'. He still calls sharks 'man-eaters' when even the local paper has stopped using that term and a big bold typeface every time a local surfer or skindiver is killed. Ironically, it was on Dad's watch that the conservation tide turned and people started holding demonstrations to save the shark. 'God's beautiful toothy creatures' was his not-for-publication expression for them.

Mack also has a special beef about media interviews with the families of shark victims: 'They always say, "Dad would've wanted to go that way." *I don't think so.* Did Dad really want to be torn in half by a great white? My guess is Dad was hoping to pass away quietly in bed at age ninety-six.'

Presumably like our father was hoping for. Not while playing the ninth hole at the Margaret River Golf Club at sixty-six.

As for my killer-whale sighting, I didn't argue with Mack. They could be swimming anywhere, I thought, north or south. Who knew what the ocean temperatures were doing these days? Anyway, it was the whale migration season and, yes, the humpbacks were heading back to the Antarctic in a daily procession after calving off the Kimberley coast over winter. So I left it at that. But a moment later I saw two creatures with rounded and shiny black backs roll out of the waves again, heading south.

They were smaller than whales but fatter and darker than dolphins. Their dorsal fins were sharply etched. And they weren't breaching like whales or smacking the water with their tails, not showing off like adolescent boys. A flock of seabirds darted and dived around them. Crested terns. So whatever species they were, they were feeding. Terns don't follow humpbacks because humpbacks eat krill, which is of no interest to terns. Like great whites, killer whales follow the humpbacks and bite chunks out of them. There's plenty of meat residue and little fish in the water.

'They're definitely killer whales,' I said. 'Two or three of them. Orcas.'

And then Mack saw them, but he still wasn't prepared to admit they were orcas. Killer whales.

'Something's out there,' he said. 'But killer whales hang out in the Southern Ocean, off Tasmania or the Canadian coast, places like that.' I knew he was thinking of the movie *Free Willy* we saw as kids. Icy waters. Oregon pines. And a tame orca like a puppy, not a wolf of the sea.

I was going to disagree but then the killer whales disappeared around the headland and Mack said, 'Forget bloody killer whales. We've got to talk about the funeral.'

We were staying for the weekend with our mother at our parents' new home, the sea-change retirement cottage they'd long planned for, to console her and discuss the arrangements for our father's funeral. Particularly the extent of the government's involvement, and how much of an official ceremony Dad was entitled to.

He'd died on Wednesday night and we were still waiting to hear from some government protocol officer whether a former minister for the environment would receive a state funeral in St George's Cathedral in Perth, with speeches and important guests, maybe including the prime minister. And, with the current political stalemate in Canberra, whether the PM and perhaps some cabinet ministers would bother to fly all the way to Western

Australia for the funeral of a former environment minister. Not treasurer or minister for home affairs or defence or anything like that.

There was a lot to discuss. Especially with our grieving mother not making much sense. In between sobs and brave smiles and narcoleptic episodes at the dinner table she was advocating a small, private, family-only affair one minute, then switching to wanting a state funeral with all the bells and whistles the next. It was as if her dead husband lying in a country-town undertaker's was two different people. She kept moaning about Adam and Alisha, too, which jangled our nerves.

'At last I can speak freely,' she whispered to me at one stage before dozing off again. I noticed Dad's single-malt stocks had taken a hammering. To be fair, Mack may have been partly responsible for that.

Obviously Dad's death had made her think about death and family sadness in general, mostly of Adam dying back in 2005, when he was only twenty-eight. And Alisha's accident before that, in 1994. The tragedies of our big brother and little sister.

It's over twenty years ago now but it still shocks me to remember hearing that Alisha had shot herself in the spine while rabbit hunting with Dad and Adam in the bush paddocks behind the Duncans' Rosella Hills vineyard.

How did she manage to do that? Apparently she was climbing through a barbwire fence and somehow the .22 she was carrying got caught up in the wire and she shot herself in the back. She was only twelve, so those of us who weren't there that afternoon put it down to her youth and inexperience. Mack and I thought, but didn't say (we *couldn't* say), *What was a small skinny girl doing in charge of a rifle?*

Anyway, from that afternoon Alisha was a paraplegic, and despite her accident, or maybe because of it, she bravely 'made something of herself', as Dad put it, studying science at UWA and doing well, and becoming a research scientist in the important fields of water engineering and groundwater studies.

She played wheelchair basketball at a top level. And in life generally she also spun around recklessly in small circles, and kept smiling, although the smile was sometimes more of a grimace, and the veins in her neck stood out and her face got red and her eyes rolled back when she had phantom pains down her legs.

And Adam? At eighteen he was already a drinker and chain-smoker and carouser. Soon, a big gambler, popular with the bookies. A classic bachelor. Nightclubs. Girls galore. Coke, too. Loads of similar gung-ho friends. For ten years he lived like there was no tomorrow.

Sadly, for him there wasn't. Although it was a surprise when his heart gave out so young, it wasn't a *huge* surprise.

Of us three boys and a girl, Adam was the child everyone said was most like our father in personality. Dad was a self-made man, as they used to call people like him. A successful builder and developer and investor: revered occupations in a West Australian boom. A hearty, blustery, stiff-drinking, sailing, golfing, fishing and shooting sort of man, with a network of important friends. And then a politician, too, winning preselection for a marginal seat. Still more mates in high places then, including the federal government.

In the swing to the conservatives he scraped into parliament, surprising everybody, including his party. And after managing to retain his seat with increased majorities in the next two elections he was rewarded in the state-by-state ministry carve-up with the environment portfolio.

Dad in charge of the environment? Some people, especially the Opposition, laughed at that: a bulldozing developer – a former swamp drainer and tree remover – running greenish matters. Not someone you'd think would be the saviour of the alpine echidna and the Bromley's speckled froglet. Or the great white shark. But he relished being a minister, and everything that went with it. He even stared down the big mining companies occasionally.

This particular Sunday when Mack and I returned from The Shelter, Mum greeted us surprisingly brightly at the cottage door. She'd put on fresh make-up and I guessed she was on sedatives or alcohol because there was lipstick on her teeth and she began firing off questions like bullets. She was anxious to know what the new restaurant was like, and what we'd eaten, and whether they served gluten-free and vegetarian options, or was it just fish, and was there a good view?

'A great view.' I told her of the killer whales. 'Quite a surprise to me,' I said. 'If not to Mack.'

'We're thinking of eating there soon,' she said gaily, and then remembered she wasn't a 'we' any more. And she had to sit down.

'Alisha will be here shortly,' she said then, and blinked as if to clear her head, and put her glasses on and took them off, and while we waited for Alisha to arrive in her specially adapted Subaru, my mother declared again, defiantly this time, 'I can speak freely now.'

'Freely about what, Mum?'

She looked at me sternly. 'Wait until Alisha arrives.'

When Alisha turned up, and had barely got out of her car, and we'd unfolded her wheelchair and she'd made it to the verandah, my mother announced to her, to our surprise, 'I've made a decision. We're eating at The Shelter tonight. There's no food in the house anyway, and the boys tell me it's a fabulous restaurant. Not to be missed.'

Alisha looked at us. Mack and I shrugged. Two meals there in a row?

'Okay,' everyone said.

'Apparently you can see killer whales there,' Mum informed us. 'Thingamajigs. Orcas.'

We noticed Dad's golf clubs were still on the Range Rover's back seat. 'We won't use your father's car,' she insisted. 'Not tonight.'

The sun was just setting when we arrived at the restaurant. We were the first diners of the evening and the wait staff, a blond youth and an ornately tattooed girl with two oceans and a tropical island spread across her back and shoulders, were surprised to see Mack and me back again.

'I'm here to see the killer whales,' Mum said.

'What killer whales?' the waiters said, and looked at each other, and at us, and Mack gave them a confiding wink.

'We'll see what we can do,' said the girl, and showed us to the same table overlooking the ocean.

The sea breeze had dropped and the ocean rolled calm and slick all the way to the horizon and beyond. It was too early to be dining and low pink sunrays slanted across our table and shone in our cutlery. Our mother took control of the wine list, and without asking our preferences (and disregarding her own fondness for chardonnay) she ordered the sort of heavy red that Dad and his business and political cronies used to favour.

This evening we were giving her leeway about everything. She was a new widow after all. 'This is what he would be drinking if he was here this evening,' she said firmly, as if that settled it. 'He would be sitting there,' she went on, indicating the vacant chair at the head of the table that all of us had avoided, as if we were deferentially saving it for him. 'And he'd be drinking this. And holding forth, of course.'

And then she raised her voice and said, 'And I wouldn't be brave enough to say what has been troubling me ever since Adam died.' At this stage a tremble came into her words, and she wiped her eyes and reached out and put a hand on Alisha's shoulder, although she wasn't looking at her.

'Alisha didn't shoot herself. Adam shot her accidentally. He tripped. And Dad switched the rifles around. Alisha's terrible misfortune was bad enough, he said. He told me he didn't want Adam to suffer any more punishment than he'd be suffering already. And Adam certainly did suffer ever after.'

She took a sip of wine and went on. 'Dad said a shooting accident wasn't good for any politician. Even though he was going after rabbits, he thought a gun-toting environment minister was politically unpalatable. So was a twelve-year-old daughter going shooting. And her climbing under a barbwire fence with a loaded gun was really bad news. But the fact that she'd shot herself was the best and most sympathetic option in the circumstances. For the public and the media. There would be sympathy for Alisha and for the family.'

Alisha made one of her fierce grimaces, and shook her head and went all wall-eyed. It was frightening to see.

Mum went on, squeezing Alisha's shoulder while she addressed the table. 'You weren't to know that the bullet came from elsewhere. While Adam never let on, he never recovered from the guilt. In the end it did him in.'

I wasn't sure if Alisha's contorted expression was from the regular ghost pains in her legs or if she was in savage disagreement with our mother.

'Jesus!' Alisha exploded then. Mum removed her hand from her shoulder. And the words burst out of our sister.

'Dad insisted on taking us shooting in the bush in the late afternoon. After lunch! He and Adam were firing away at rabbits. Dad had had his usual few glasses of wine and he sort of stumbled on something and shot me. I'm sure of that. In his panic that day he must've immediately told Adam that he'd done it. Then he thought it over and told the police and the world I'd got tangled up in the fence and shot myself. No one questioned him – he was a minister.

Adam always thought guiltily that this version had saved his bacon, and he felt guilty ever after. I wasn't conscious enough to disagree. And Adam and I were forbidden to speak of that afternoon again.'

We sat there at the table, no one speaking, as the sun sank below the horizon and the pink and gold streaks faded from the sky and the restaurant's lights came on and the geographically tattooed waitress brought us water and asked for our orders.

'Did you hear me, Mum?' Alisha said, in the calmest manner, and took a long sip of wine. 'Were you even listening? My father shot me.'

My mother was yawning in the odd way she had before a narcoleptic episode. If you weren't watching her, she could go face-down into the soup. I nudged her and she blinked several times and put on her glasses and took them off again.

'Where are those killer whales anyway?' she asked the waitress in her new bossy widow's voice.

We all stared out to sea. The four of us, and the two waiters as well, frowning and searching the horizon. Time passed and no one spoke. But in the whole panorama of the darkening Indian Ocean there was nothing to be seen.

Imaginary Islands

On their island honeymoon, David Lang remembered, they'd disagreed first over a flea she said she spotted on the hotel bed, then a jellyfish sting and Byron swimming the Hellespont.

The flea on the bedspread had sent Angela into a panic the moment they entered their room. She refused to even sip the champagne he'd organised until he phoned 'for someone to hunt it down'.

David examined the bed and shook the coverlet with an elaborate flourish. Her flea anxiety was disappointing and embarrassing. He didn't want anything as silly as a flea to mar their honeymoon. It was kind of ridiculous. He couldn't spot anything, and said so. Fancy her being troubled by a flea – an alleged flea – at a time like this!

But she was definitely agitated. 'They jump, you know. What sort of hotel is this, with fleas in the bed?'

'Flea singular,' he said. 'Maybe.' He gave a nervous laugh. 'Anyway, if there was one, it's gone now.' He put his arms around her.

Her shoulders were tense and she wriggled away. For the wedding the hairdresser had done something unfamiliar with her hair that he thought looked complicated and ancient. Maybe Egyptian. He preferred her dark hair long and simple. She said, 'Where there's one there's always hundreds.'

'Really? I don't think so.'

But her insistence that he summon someone to catch and kill it, that she couldn't possibly relax with a flea lurking in the marriage bed, ready to spring out and bite her, with her 'serious insect allergies' (which came as news to him), made him complain to Housekeeping.

The flea was long gone, of course, if indeed it had existed. The housekeeper rolled her eyes and said it was probably just a spot or thread on the coverlet. The woman departed the unsuccessful flea hunt in a miasma of insect repellent and with a sarcastic, 'I'll leave the spray can with you. Better luck with the rest of your honeymoon.'

They had to walk on the beach while the smelly cloud disappeared. It was a silent walk. He'd never seen Angela rant before. He put it down to wedding nerves. She still had the complicated Egyptian hairstyle, which looked even stranger with casual clothes. David wondered whether she or her hairdresser, Hans of Vienna, had been thinking Elizabeth Taylor in *Cleopatra*.

Perhaps the insecticide had done its work and, eventually, the champagne, because the total absence of fleas allowed the marriage to be consummated and the honeymoon to proceed in a normal manner until Angela was stung on the thigh while wading in Thomson Bay two afternoons later.

She shrieked and sobbed. If he'd thought her flea outburst a little excessive, the anxiety she now displayed at a tiny transparent stinger leaving a faint pink welt on her leg was, in his opinion, definitely overdramatic. Marine stings were a normal expectation on the Australian coast. Who hadn't been stung by a bluebottle some time? Even half-hearted dog-paddlers like Angela. Sure, it could hurt, but every beachgoer had their own home remedy, whether vinegar, hot water, iced water, beer, even – so some old codgers said – urine. You winced, treated the sting if necessary, and got over it.

But she was moaning that it was agony. 'David, I can't walk!' So to the startled glances of holidaymakers, he lifted up his new bride, hoisted her on his back, and carried her up from the shore towards the tearooms. The sign there said *Sandwiches-Hamburgers-Hot Water*. The hot water was for people who drank tea, tea being more popular than coffee back then. 'Hot water's the best cure,' he muttered to her.

There was no breeze, the summer sun bore down and crows and bush flies mocked their progress. His sweat made her a slippery burden. Encumbered, he couldn't brush the sticky relentless flies from his face.

'No, I need a hospital!' Angela cried, so he changed course, veered through the crowded settlement to more curious and amused stares, and piggybacked her to the medical hut. She was still moaning as he set her down and the nurse bathed her leg in vinegar and water.

'You're my fifth case today,' the nurse said. 'Of course the others were just little kids.'

'Hospital is what I need,' Angela kept insisting. 'A proper hospital – Royal Perth. I need an emergency flight. Take me to the airport, David.'

'Are you serious, love?' the nurse wondered, giving her two Panadols. 'The plane's for actual emergencies. In an hour you'll feel better. Have a lie-down.'

'This *is* an emergency,' Angela said.

In this second, more serious disagreement of their honeymoon, he declared, 'Angela, the nurse is right. Please come and rest and calm down.' He hoisted her up again and carried her, still protesting, back to their room, where he collapsed in a pool of sweat and she lay on the bed facing the wall and woke an hour later morosely but miraculously healed.

The Byron argument had begun harmlessly enough next day. He'd waded ashore over the reef after swimming the channel at the Basin. Since the sting Angela wasn't venturing out more than ankle-deep. She was sitting warily on the shoreline as the tide lapped at her feet, and with cupped hands she was splashing water over her body like an elderly non-swimmer, like someone's wary immigrant grandmother from an ancient landlocked country, not a twenty-year-old West Australian girl in a blue bikini.

'Heroic Lord Byron returns from swimming the Hellespont,' David joked, flicking water at her. She was a bookish girl, hence the bookish reference to impress her. He didn't have many of them.

'Byron was always showing off,' Angela said.

'A good swimmer, though,' he said, reaching for a towel.

'Not as good as Shelley.'

'You're kidding! Shelley couldn't swim a stroke! That's why he drowned.'

'Shelley loved the water. He worshipped the water and found it erotic and lyrical. I did Shelley at school.'

'But he couldn't swim in it. When his boat sank it was curtains for Shelley. His body washed up on the beach and was cremated there. And his heart didn't burn. That was weird. And didn't his wife write *Frankenstein*?' This, rather than his poetry, was the sum of his Shelley knowledge.

'He was better than Byron, anyway.'

'Not at swimming.'

'If you insist. But at poetry.'

He spread out the towel and lay on his back in the sun. 'Okay,' he said, and closed his eyes and the kaleidoscopic shapes did their customary dance behind his eyelids. He'd done Byron at school. The bored surfing boys in English class had perked up at the references to swimming and sex and dashing behaviour. The mad, bad and dangerous-to-know stuff. The club foot and the half-sister got their attention. Byron was always at it. He preferred Byron.

And now he was a married man.

*

The island loomed sharply into view as David Lang sat drinking a beer on the balcony of the Airbnb apartment he'd rented in Perth for the holidays. He was long divorced from Angela, presently living alone in Sydney since the break-up with Victoria, and it was the evening of Christmas Day. He was expecting his children and grandchildren for dinner and his mind at the moment was in a place with vivid family memories because only a hundred metres along the beachfront was the Seaview Hotel where their father had taken them to Christmas dinner six months after their mother died.

Forty-nine years ago, and of all his childhood Christmases he remembered this one the clearest. He recalled the heat of the sun on his shoulders as they got out of the car, the bitumen bubbling in the hotel car park, the hibiscuses wilting around a sandy patch of buffalo grass out front, and the stale beer and floor-polish smell in the hotel corridors.

Their table ('the best in the dining room', their father had said proudly) faced the ocean. The sea was grey and sullen and windless all the way to the western horizon, and stretching north and south as well. It was the first time he'd considered Rottnest Island as a moving mirage, mysteriously appearing miles from its true position. The real island had been erased and where it belonged was now bare ocean. In the heat haze beyond the dining-room window, three separate islands – smoky, shimmering landmasses – sailed southwards.

He was eleven, suddenly feeling too old for the Biggles and Famous Five books he'd received as gifts, sweltering in his school uniform and self-conscious in his stupid party hat. They'd always worn them at home after pulling the Christmas crackers, but that was fun and this was different and Dad was behaving as if it wasn't different. Wearing a mauve crepe-paper crown with a jaunty air and the dye beginning to trickle down his damp forehead, his father was loud and embarrassing and the whole thing was wrong.

He recalled the hotel manageress joining them at their table after the plum pudding, and his and Max's and Annie's surprise when this woman they'd never met had gifts for them, important-looking presents wrapped in gold paper. Fountain pens for him and Max. A bride doll for Annie. The manageress wore strong perfume and red lipstick and from the way she mopped Dad's brow with a napkin she seemed to know him well. She brought him and herself brandies and called him Rex, not Mr Lang.

'Get some fresh air, kids,' Dad said, 'while I do the bill.' A cigar appeared from nowhere, and she lit it for him.

As they headed back to the car they snatched off their party hats in a simultaneous impulse, crumpled them and threw them on the asphalt. The inside of the Ford was stifling and the seats were hot on their legs. Max said, 'Shit! Give me air!' and Max and he tore off their ties and school shoes, and Annie tossed the doll into the back and took off her patent-leather party shoes and frilly socks, and everyone groaned in an exaggerated way. He knew they were all thinking of past Christmases at home. But no one cried.

As they wound down the car windows they could see into the manageress's office. She was combing Dad's hair where his party hat had tousled it, and he was grinning. They all looked away uncomfortably. Eyes front. No one spoke.

Across the ocean horizon in front of them, the three displaced and imaginary islands with their phantom trees and ghostly mountains kept sailing further and further south in the grey sea.

*

This Christmas evening, however, Rottnest Island was in correct order both optically and geographically. A single island perfectly *in situ* on the horizon. Due west as expected. Its outline sharply defined. Both lighthouses visible. Everything as it should be. Next stop Africa.

These days there were annual swimming races from the mainland to the island. Events far further and more adventurous than Byron's one-mile Hellespont crossing. Twenty kilometres of open ocean, with shipping traffic and hypothermia and stingers and even seasickness from the ocean swells. And so many swimmers were keen to participate that the organisers had to hold a ballot for entrants. Some swimmers, men and women both, were so fit and enthusiastic that when they reached the island they turned around and swam back.

In the week since David had arrived in Perth he'd noticed a young woman in a black racing swimsuit stride down to the water an hour before sunset each evening. From the balcony he watched her drop her blue striped towel on the sand, tuck her long dark hair into a yellow cap, march into the water, dive under the shore break and swim vigorously out to sea. She swam beyond the outer surf line and marker buoys, so far out that he eventually lost sight of her cap.

Her disappearance made him slightly anxious the first evening. But as the sun began its descent into the horizon, he spotted a small line of splashes appear and grow bigger and there she was, stroking neatly back to shore, her evening exercise perfectly timed to the last vestiges of daylight. As the red whale dived into the golden sea, she strode ashore, took off her cap, shook out her hair, dried herself with the blue striped towel, and left the beach in the approaching twilight.

But last night, Christmas Eve, as she completed her swim and neared the beach at sunset, she'd removed the cap while still knee-deep in the sea. Then she swung a heavy fall of hair in his direction and lowered it into the water. Could she see him on the balcony watching her? Had she spotted him on the six previous nights? He wondered this but couldn't turn away or stop looking at her. She straightened up, still facing him, briskly gathered up her hair and squeezed out the water.

Then for some reason, as if acting on a sudden impulse, she smiled widely and repeated this display. With a wide looping action she dropped her blanket of hair in the sea again, a shining black cascade in the setting sun, and then straightened up and flung it in a sweep of sparkling droplets. The darkening silhouette of the island was behind her as she bowed her head towards him on the balcony and caught her waterfall of hair in her arms, and threw it back.

David felt his face go hot with embarrassment at being spotted, but also with appreciation of her Christmas Eve poise and her teasing performance. Smooth-haired now, sleek and athletic in her black swimsuit, she strode boldly up the sand, gathered up her towel and was gone.

On Christmas night she was there again at the usual time. Before his family arrived he was on the balcony to watch her ocean entrance as usual, her confident plunge through the breakers, the yellow cap bobbing in the swell. Since the night before he had felt a pride in her self-assurance and, yes, a definite connection between them. Strangely, as if they were in this experience together.

Inside again, making dinner preparations, he heard voices below the balcony reminding him of the new community habit in full swing. West Australians now celebrated their Indian Ocean sunsets. After a hot summer day the coastal cliffs attracted lines of sightseers, especially young people, drawn to view the dazzling conjoined spectacle of sky and sea.

On this special holiday, the crowds of sunset lovers were defying the local authorities' laws against public drinking to praise the blazing sky with beer and wine. But even at Christmas there seemed a solemnity rather than a party atmosphere about them.

When the sun finally ended the lightshow by submerging dramatically into the sea he heard respectful cheers and whistles along the seafront. He couldn't remember anyone acknowledging the sunset in his youth, much less applauding it. Sunset as entertainment – such a simple, wondrous and inexpensive pleasure. He wished he was twenty again and cheering the sunset with a beer and a pretty and understanding girl. Maybe a sunset ocean swimmer like the bold black-haired girl.

Welcoming the first arrivals for dinner, his daughter Helena and her children, Harrison and Scarlett, ten and eight, he remarked on the phenomenon of the sunset-watchers. 'Yes, yes,'

Helena said briskly. 'Gorgeous, isn't it?' Her body felt strangely bony and reduced when he embraced her.

Scarlett's eyes darted about and found the small artificial Christmas tree he'd bought. 'Presents?' she said archly.

'I said to wait,' her mother said.

'Wait, wait, wait,' sighed Scarlett.

'When everyone arrives, sweetheart,' said their grandfather.

'Isn't this the beach where people were attacked by sharks?' said Harrison. Their eyes lit up in the hope this was presently occurring and the children ran out to the balcony.

'Not *attacked* – *bitten.* It's not like the sharks committed a crime,' their mother called after them. She was ferrying bowls into the kitchen – two big and imaginative salads involving tofu, nuts, leaves, seeds, stems, peels and many shades of green and orange. 'And a long time ago.'

As David expected, Helena's husband Nigel was a no-show. Details were vague, but according to her, his son-in-law had returned to Hong Kong, his old home, 'to sort out the family finances'.

Apparently Nigel's brother Dominic had either done something complex with the Chan companies or had failed to do something complex, she wasn't sure which. Anyway, it was a serious financial misjudgement that needed Nigel Chan's superior knowledge of auditors' reports, or whatever. She said he'd been too busy to explain or to communicate much lately.

Nigel had now been gone three months, and Helena looked older, harried and gaunt and she showed half an inch of dark hair below the dyed blondness that her father hadn't noticed before. David didn't know if this was an intentional hairstyle or negligence, just as he wasn't sure whether her new thinness was the result of recently turning vegan or due to anxiety over her husband's continuing absence. Maybe both.

No attempt by Nigel to make it back for Christmas? David thought this was wrong of him, and deeply hurtful to Helena and the kids. Hong Kong to Perth was only seven-and-a-half hours. The same time zone. However, he didn't bring this up with her at this point. Not at Christmas. Why disturb her more?

'I got some seafood,' he told her. 'Perfect for a hot evening.'

'For you and Paul, maybe,' she said. 'The kids won't touch it. And as I keep saying till I'm blue in the face, I'm a vegan.'

'I thought maybe crustaceans might slip through your net. As a lower form of creature. No actual mammals slaughtered.'

'I don't think you get it, Dad.'

'I thought it was mainly mammals and not wearing leather.'

Out on the balcony, Scarlett shouted, 'I saw a fin!'

'No, she didn't,' said Harrison. He came inside and slumped down with his phone. 'I'm hungry,' he whined.

Were the kids vegans as well? their grandfather wondered. They looked chubbier than ever.

'I've got some ham, too,' he said. 'Paul is bringing the cold turkey,' he said.

'How appropriate,' Helena muttered.

Even twenty years later she couldn't resist a crack about her older brother. One Friday night in the pub when he was nineteen

Paul been arrested in a police sting with a small amount of cocaine, sold to him five minutes earlier.

'Something nice for Happy Hour,' the dealer said, winking at the plainclothes men at the bar. They'd nabbed a dozen boys in half an hour. He pleaded guilty, received a six-month good-behaviour bond for possession and was spared a conviction.

That close shave was enough for him, Paul said. 'The first and only drug experiment,' he assured his shocked parents. 'I'm not into anything. Not even grass.'

'Nonsense,' said his younger sister. She'd been on his case since he was fifteen. 'You and your constant cones. You forget we had adjoining bedrooms. You are such a bullshitter.'

'Just a few ciggies at parties and weekends.'

There was no credit coming from his father either. David was just as opposed to ordinary cigarettes. 'Cigarettes killed Grandpa Rex,' he'd been telling his children ever since primary school. His lectures had begun early. He wanted to catch them before the teenage desperate-to-be-cool stage.

'Seventy unfiltered a day at his peak. And cigars too,' he told them. Rex used to light one Turf from another, usually had one on the go, another resting in the ashtray near his drink and one burning a hole on the edge of the dresser. His early-morning coughing fit was a legend in their street and he was dead at fifty-seven.

And still Paul had taken no notice. Or had he? After years of parental nagging, Paul nowadays insisted he'd given up tobacco. His new job as an Uber driver forbade stinking vehicles so he'd taken up electronic cigarettes. A battery-powered device that heated liquid into an aerosol vapour that you inhaled into your lungs! A pretend cigarette! An e-cig! Vaping! His father was speechless.

And this Christmas evening Paul arrived at the family dinner with a turducken and a bar attendant from the Seaview Hotel in a bikini top and extremely short denim shorts.

'This is my friend Skye. And, *tah-dah,* this is a turkey that's been stuffed with a duck, then the duck was stuffed with a chicken.'

Skye planted a juicy kiss on David's cheek. 'Welcome,' he murmured to this woman he'd never met before. He was bewildered on several fronts. *A tur-what? And you might have mentioned you were bringing someone!*

Helena said, 'Poultry gross-out! She was eyeing Skye's shaved head and upper-breast tattoos of Hawaiian scenes. 'I can't believe you, Paul.'

'Chill. Merry Christmas.'

David rallied with a laugh. 'Why stop at a turkey? Why not a goose?'

'Or try an emu at the top end,' said Helena. 'And a budgie at the bottom.'

'They don't ram a whole chicken up the duck's bum, and so forth,' Paul said defensively. 'They're deboned.'

'They're a big thing in America,' Skye offered. 'For Thanksgiving.'

Paul said, 'And becoming popular here as well. I've been delivering them all over town for Uber Eats. You can get them with quails too, at the starting point, under the chicken. But they'd sold out of those.'

'Turduckenquails?' David wondered.

'Four bird roast,' corrected his son. 'What are we drinking, Dad? Skye likes cocktails. I might make some daiquiris.'

'Isn't it time for presents yet?' moaned Scarlett and Harrison together.

*

It was the senior Langs' habit for their children to have Christmas lunch at Angela's house and the evening meal with David. Minus the other parent on each occasion.

David and Angela only communicated rarely and indirectly nowadays. Angela's husband Warren Lutz, managing director of Lutz Toyota Osborne Park, discouraged it, which was fine with David after several uncomfortable family gatherings where conversation lapsed into indignant silence once he declared that he personally viewed cars as 'just a means of getting from A to B', and 'a useful piece of machinery, like a fridge or a toaster'.

The evening dinner necessitated weary adults and grizzling grandchildren staying up later and forcing down more Christmas fare than they needed, but the fact that he'd flown across the country to spend Christmas with them carried some emotional weight.

So the habit continued this year, except for Tim's absence. At the last moment he'd announced a skiing holiday in Aspen with 'Taylor', apparently another young Sydney barrister. The family had only learned of Taylor's existence in the past fortnight, and no one had met Taylor, who was 'just a friend' and 'a very private person' and there was 'no need at this stage for family stuff'.

Disappointed more than he let on at Tim's non-appearance, David tried unsuccessfully to imagine a shy Sydney barrister and kept thinking how *Taylor* was a unisex name.

These days whenever he saw his children after an absence, especially as they grew older, he found himself searching their faces for his own features. Disappointingly, he recognised Angela's in them more often than his own. Maybe he didn't really know what he looked like. But not only was he now fascinated by genetics generally, he wanted his children to resemble him more.

Tonight, with her new vegan gauntness, he saw versions of his nose and eye circles in Helena for the first time. But she still had Angela's chin and mouth, her (originally) dark hair (they'd all inherited that), her propensity for hypochondria and hurt feelings (and the sulks that followed) and her way of presenting her wishes and opinion as an ultimatum. Her way or the highway. Except if it involved Nigel Chan. Nigel's way overruled.

And Paul? His head slick with hair product tonight, he looked like neither of his parents. Sipping his daiquiri, he looked like his grandfather, like Brylcreemed Rex Lang circa 1960. The devoted attention to his hair. The same roguish gap between the front teeth. (Clark Gable teeth, Rex used to insist, to his wife's scoffing.) The same need to inhale drugs.

Genes will out, David thought. For the first time in his life he was curious about his ancestors, too, as well as his descendants. A sign of advancing age, he supposed, like thinking of religion for the first time and seeing the point of church. When he was young and had the chance to inquire about his forebears, easily done when his parents and grandparents were alive, he'd never once asked them. He couldn't care less where they came from. He lived in the *now*. He lived for the beach and the surf. As attested by the suspect scars on his face and hands and legs: the six-monthly whittling away of his ears and nose. Bad skin genes for an Australian. Sorry, children. Wear a sunhat.

But he had something to tell Paul and Helena tonight, something he thought might interest or at least amuse them. He'd recently had his ethnicity laboratory-tested by a new online company that specialised in researching ancestry. It was all the rage. They'd sent him a kit with two swabs to dab inside his cheeks, seal in the tubes provided, and return. Two months later they'd sent him his personal DNA news. It had arrived just before Christmas.

'Guess what?' he said now. 'I'm thirty-eight per cent English, thirty-six per cent Irish, eighteen per cent French and German and eight per cent Finnish.'

'And?' said Helena.

'So that's *your* background, too – or half of it.'

'It's only half yours, actually,' Helena said. 'Because they can only test mitochondrial DNA from the mother's side.'

'It sounds pretty dull except for the Finnish,' Paul said. 'Are we talking vodka lovers and Vikings?'

'I used to go with a Swedish boy,' said Skye. 'Blond hair and beard, six-foot-six. Thor really had the whole Viking thing going on.'

Helena laughed. 'Thor? You're kidding.'

'Did you know him too?'

David broke in. 'So, Paul. What's been happening with you lately?' Something involving Skye, obviously. 'Apart from giving up smoking at last?'

Skye answered for him. 'Not just the smoking. I've got him on a great health and relaxation kick. Tai chi and float tanks. Notice how serene your son is.'

'Until last Thursday anyway,' said Paul.

'Oh, I forgot.' Skye shook her head. 'Don't say it.'

'So there I am on Thursday,' he went on regardless. 'Floating naked in the pitch dark, in a warm-water tank of Epsom salts.'

'More like a tomb,' Helena butted in. 'I've seen them.'

'Anyway,' said Paul, 'soft music's playing. It's my fourth or fifth time floating, and I'm used to it now. It's not claustrophobic any more, it's very relaxing, and when I get out, there'll be a cup of calming herbal tea waiting.'

'Uh-huh,' Skye muttered.

'And I'm floating away, totally peaceful, half-asleep and hassle-free, and I feel something bump against my thigh in the dark. And bump again. For a second I think I'm floating in the sea and it's a fish.'

Skye had her head in her hands.

'But it wasn't a fish.' Paul was relishing the story now. 'It was a turd!'

The reaction was as expected: disgust and shocked laughter.

Paul sipped his drink, oddly debonair, Rex to a tee. 'It just proved how relaxed the person floating before me must have been.'

*

David rose on a fine Boxing Day to the smell of frying ham and coffee and clattering in the kitchen. Paul and Skye had stayed the night to avoid the booze bus, and they were cooking breakfast.

'The best part of Christmas is the ham for breakfast for days afterwards,' said David.

Paul said, 'And the before-breakfast swim to cure the hangover. Ready to go, Dad?'

Father and son crossed the road to the beach. How long had it been since he and Paul had swum or surfed together, David wondered. Five or six years? Always a real enjoyment to him ever since the boy was four or five and he'd carry him, shrieking with pleasure, on his back into shore, his 'Daddy surfboard'. Then there were the competitive teen years when Paul gradually overcame him as a surfer and swimmer (the huge effort he put into beating his father!) and David hardly begrudged this happening.

Already there was activity on the shore – people bobbing in the waves, men on surf skis, and racing children trying out their Christmas beach toys.

David saw it as soon as they set foot on the sand. The blue striped towel. But was it hers? It looked to be in the same spot she'd left it the night before, but he couldn't quite remember because of course the tide had since come in and out.

She must be having a morning swim today. He looked out to sea. The windless ocean was glassy all the way to Rottnest and the horizon. There was no sign of the yellow cap.

He hadn't been on the balcony last night to oversee her return. Guiltily, he walked up to the towel and nudged it with his foot.

Sand had blown onto it and weighed it down. It was slightly damp. Rolled into a corner of the towel was a set of car keys.

David had a brief swim to clear his head. He needed to think, but he felt breathless in the surf. Paul caught a couple of waves and came ashore, too.

'That's better,' Paul said. 'Let's go, Dad. Skye's holding breakfast.'

David sat down by the blue striped towel, his eyes fixed on the wide ocean and the island beyond. 'I need to wait here,' he said.

the True Colour of the Sea

Long before he'd put brush to canvas he had a title for the painting. *Searching the Horizon at Sunset in the Hope of Seeing a Vessel in the Arafura Sea.* He was on the cliff every afternoon and into the evening, watching the sun sinking like a crimson whale, the sky streaking mauve and orange, the vast empty ocean darkening all around. How could he call it anything else?

Before the painting was half done he finished his last block of indigo. Of course he'd brought his paintbox of watercolours with him, with enough indigo for the three days, he'd reasoned. Even for several seascapes. But as it turned out, sunsets in the Arafura Sea required a lot of indigo, and layering the paint, or mixing cobalt and violet, didn't work at all. Add a spot of black for the ocean, the merest drop, and you ended up with sludge like the colour of the mangrove mudflats.

Rather than a seascape, this painting was turning into a bad self-portrait. Not since the Royal Academy ten years before had he been his own subject. In a flurry of despair he imagined the critics' judgement: *Zachary Nash's first self-portrait since his student days is a dubious study in solitude. How saddening it is to recall that first brilliant exhibition at the age of fifteen. Alas, early promise seems unfulfilled.*

Well, that's what they'd say if there were any critics here to pass artistic sentence. Or any back in mainland Australia, for that matter.

Of course he was his own harshest critic and his thoughts were all over the place. He wasn't himself, whatever that was these days. Surely nothing more ridiculous existed in art or life than this half-finished stick figure reclining on a rock and staring mournfully out at an uncertain sea.

Even worse than a suspect study in solitude was a study of extreme self-pity. A better title would be *Pathetic Artist Cringing Against a Sullen Backdrop.* God, he was twenty-five and the figure he'd painted looked like a London street urchin! Better still, *Starving Dickensian Orphan with Dog Overlooking Murky Ocean.*

Without a mirror he'd drawn himself from memory, taking into account his present condition (but eliminating the beard). Of course his clothes hung looser on him now. His body was clammy in the humidity. His gums bled. His legs had weeping sores. He always smelled of fish.

'I'm pathetic,' Zachary Nash muttered into the breeze from the western ocean. 'And I've got the bloody sea wrong!' The dog looked up worriedly for a second, then slumped down again, its muzzle buried in its paws. When a breaking wave and sudden wind gust sprayed man, animal and canvas, Nash shouted, 'Widdle! Listen to me! I'm bloody pathetic!'

Widdle stood up, stiffly and abjectly, and in four slow and rickety stages shook himself dry.

In the fading light the ocean was assuming its dominant evening shade of indigo once more. But the underwater reefs and tonight's cloud arrangements and a confluence of breezes and tides made the sea a dark and choppy patchwork. Grimmer than by day. Not for the first time, Nash considered tossing it in. Throwing everything over the cliff. But he slowly packed up his paintbox and whistled for Widdle.

Another gaudy sunset anticlimax concluded in the Arafura Sea, another vast indigo ocean uncaptured for posterity, and still no sign of the *Eileen.*

*

The *Eileen*'s departure from Broome had been determined by the tides. On the north-west coast the tidal range could be as much as thirty feet, and he drank brandy on the verandah of the Roebuck Hotel with the pearling master and the mate while they waited for the night's spring tide to turn.

Nash remembered that tropical September night as fine and clear. He recalled the breeze parting the mangroves below the pub as precisely as a comb through oiled hair. Someone was playing a piano accordion over the bar hubbub downstairs. The full moon rose over the exposed mud flats of Roebuck Bay in the reflective phenomenon the pearlers called *Staircase to the Moon*. A natural lightshow, like a ladder to heaven.

'Definitely worth painting one day,' he'd said confidently, as he showed Captain Henry Byrd his well-worn letter of introduction.

This is to introduce the important young English artist Zachary Nash R.A. whose unique body of work at home and abroad since 1889, especially paintings arising from his imaginative voyages of exploration, already comprises one of the most significant records of European contact with foreign and faraway places this century.

Nash's friendly nature, good humour and easy mode of address stand him in good stead in his travels. He mixes easily in different types of society, not only with Her Majesty's representatives in the colonies he visits, but just as readily with the tattooed Maoris of New Zealand, the gruff whaling captains of Boston or the cheerful seabird-eating inhabitants of Tasmania.

Any assistance you could provide during his travels in the colonies would be greatly appreciated.

Yours sincerely,

Gloucester.

'That's the *Duke* of Gloucester,' he told the captain. 'Nobility sign their names like that. Just the one word.'

'Is that so?' Byrd said.

'The duke's a good chum of yours?' wondered the mate.

'An art patron.' Nash slapped at a mosquito. 'An enthusiast.'

'He certainly sounds enthusiastic about you,' the mate said, and winked.

From the bar below came the sounds of breaking glass and laughter, and the accordion music came to a wheezing halt. Nash peered out over the verandah rail and beyond the mangroves to the mudflats where the tide was beginning to rush in. The incoming waves and spindrift were backlit by the moon's rays. He turned to Byrd.

'To explain myself,' he said, 'in the past few years, art has taken me to the Americas, the Caribbean, India, Mauritius, St Helena, the Pacific, New Zealand, Tasmania, New South Wales and now here to Western Australia.'

This announcement lay there for a time while the captain examined the level of brandy in his glass and the mate perused his pocket watch. Nash slapped another mosquito and the mate said, 'They love English flesh.'

'Quite a seafarer,' the captain said eventually, and sipped his brandy. Downstairs in the bar there were ironic cheers as the accordion started up again. Someone began stamping to the music. Someone picked up the tune by tapping something metal on a glass. Maybe a pearling knife.

Nash raised his voice over the clamour. 'I'd appreciate a passage with you to the Arafura Sea. I'm interested in visiting islands hitherto unseen by an artist. I've heard you sail there regularly.'

The captain shrugged. '*Islands hitherto unseen*? What do you reckon, Cribb?'

The seamen looked at each other. 'We're always visiting *hitherto unseen* islands,' the mate said. 'Less often in the cyclone season.'

'My work was recently well received in Perth,' Nash said earnestly. When he got no reaction, he went on, 'In particular a portrait of the governor's wife, Lady Robinson, picnicking in the Darling Range. He let the subject sink in. He slapped another mosquito on his arm. 'And a portrait of a Noongar chief, "King Tommy" on Mt Eliza.'

'More important friends of yours!' said Byrd, and he winked at the mate. 'Well, if you're as upstanding as everyone says, I suppose it's all right by me.'

They sailed out of the bay around eleven p.m., bound for Captain Byrd's farthest pearling grounds, 800 miles to the north-east. As well as the mate, Joseph Cribb, who doubled as ship's carpenter, and Nash and his Airedale terrier, the *Eileen* carried fresh stores and twelve backup pearl divers for Byrd's lugger fleet presently working its way up the coast.

Byrd ran twenty-two luggers, one of the biggest fleets out of Broome. Though his boats used the new canvas suits, copper helmets, heavy boots and air hoses, he still employed bare-skin Aboriginal divers where necessary. The *Eileen* was a 200-ton, 100-foot schooner that operated as a mothership to provision his fleet and transport replacement divers when his crewmen had burst their eardrums or drowned or died from decompression sickness – the 'bends' – or from shark attacks. Or from cyclones. Especially cyclones. A single storm in February 1889 had sunk three schooners and eighty luggers and drowned four hundred men.

Still, these were unsurprising, even sporadically anticipated disasters. What most offended Captain Byrd was having to replace divers because of fights and stabbings. He had no patience for any misbehaviour, insubordination or racial disharmony on board or ashore. He forbade his crews of Japanese, Malay, Dyak, Koepanger, Filipino, Chinese and Aboriginal divers from carrying pearling knives with sharp points. Indeed, when he spotted one he snapped off the point.

Any waywardness met with rough justice. Any diver sneaking ashore to a brothel, opium den or noodle-and-grog stall (or reeling back to their luggers from these haunts), much less anyone smuggling prostitutes aboard or showing signs of syphilis (Byrd examined newcomers' soles and palms for the telltale secondary white rash), was lucky to escape with instant dismissal.

Asian divers were cheap to hire and easy to replace. Of course the punishment for a man caught stealing pearls, or even a single pearl shell, was as severe as it could be.

*

Viewed from the *Eileen*'s deck on his first morning at sea, the vast breadth of the ocean and its variegated depths registered on Nash just as inspiringly as they had on his first sea journey, to America, in 1889.

He inhaled the sensual breeze and relished the tropical sun on his shoulders. It was a delight to spot the voyage's first sea creatures, cluster after cluster of mating sea snakes. As they floated languidly past, unmindful of the *Eileen*, he made quick sketches of their seductive contortions. Transported by their sexual coupling, some of them golden, others striped, the sea snakes writhed slowly together on the ocean surface like strands of Medusa's hair.

As the schooner threaded its way around the northern reefs and islands, first to Byrd's luggers in the Timor Sea pearling grounds, the ocean's colours – both the *apparent* blue of the open sea and the *supposed* greens of its shoals and shallows – intrigued

Nash yet again. He knew they only *appeared* to be blue or green. Or grey or brown, for that matter. Their colour depended on the expanse and depth of water, the sea's absorption of sunlight, the reflected sky, the position of clouds, the presence of algae and seaweed, or river run-off and storm-stirred sediment.

There was a clearly a science behind the colour of the sea, he thought. A reason for vast oceans to be blue. But then he'd noticed that the Atlantic off the east coast of the United States – certainly immense enough – actually appeared green, not blue, regardless of depth, expanse, weather or season. By the time it joined the Caribbean, however, the same Atlantic had turned navy blue! And the adjoining Caribbean was aqua through and through! How to explain all that?

Yet again Nash the painter wondered: *What's the true colour of the sea?*

At a moment when he found himself standing alongside Cribb at the stern – the mate was trolling a heavy line in the schooner's wake and had already caught a red emperor, two big Spanish mackerel and a barracuda – he asked him that very question.

'The colour of the sea?' Cribb frowned and looked at their wake streaming behind them, as if checking to make sure. 'Pretty obvious, eh, Nash? Blue in the deep, green in the shallows, grey in a storm.'

Cribb dropped the fish in the deck-wash to stay fresh until they could be cleaned and filleted, and they lay and flapped and bled on the rolling deck, and were tossed back and forth in the deck-tide, their gill workings exposed and vibrating like scarlet anemones.

Nash took the opportunity to sketch the gasping and flailing of the fish on the deck. While they were still alive and thrashing, their colours were striking. Their metallic silvers and vivid reds. The turquoise sea reaching all around. But once dead the fish soon faded. The ferociously toothy barracuda took the longest time to die and the barefoot crew giggled at its gaping jaws and kept out of its way.

*

By noon on their third day out, he'd made several sketches of one of the deckhands as the man squatted on his heels on the deck against the foremast, sorting and scraping mother-of-pearl. One big-knuckled hand wielded the paring knife, the other nonchalantly crushed the cockroaches that were attracted to the shreds of muscle left on the shells and swarming around him. A rag loincloth covered his haunches.

The seaman, Pedro Baptiste, had a scarred face and a disproportionately large head for his wiry, near-naked body, which was also crosshatched with scars. To Nash, Baptiste was a welcome subject, well worth the two English shillings he'd given him. That glistening scar ran from his forehead down his right cheek, bisecting that side of his black moustache, all the way to his chin. Nash touched his own cheek and then pointed at Baptiste's face.

Baptiste grinned far and wide. Silver teeth gleamed. He slanted his eyes with his fingers, then he held his arms apart to simulate the length of a weapon and made a violent slashing motion. As if with a machete, Nash presumed.

This mimed interaction by the deckhand was observed by the captain as he took over the schooner's wheel from Cribb. 'What exactly is our artist passenger doing over there?' he asked the mate.

'All morning he's been sketching that ugly Filipino,' said Cribb. 'He gave him money.'

'He paid him? Not a portrait I'd want hanging over my fireplace,' said the captain.

'A change from drawing dead mackerel,' Cribb said.

In the afternoon, for another shilling, Nash sketched Baptiste again, this time while he was coiling rope, his wide feet and stocky bowlegs balancing him against the rolling slope of the deck and the heightened, windblown waves. The other crewmen laughed shrilly and called out insults, but judging by his silver grin Baptiste seemed to be enjoying the artist's attention.

*

In the Arafura Sea pearling grounds next evening, Captain Byrd surprised Nash over the dinner table with a question about art. He looked unsettled and Nash put it down to the whisky he'd been drinking since the afternoon.

'I've been thinking,' Byrd said. 'In my old sailor's ignorance, I seem to have got it all wrong. I thought art was about beauty.'

'Art is certainly about beauty,' Nash said.

'Because of my seagoing profession,' the captain went on, 'my wife likes books with pictures by the English artist named Turner. And I can see why she regards that fellow's paintings as things of beauty.'

'Indeed they are. And they have a personal appeal to you?'

'Yes, Turner's artistic efforts remind me of my own evenings at sea. Storms and coasts I've experienced myself. I must say the man knows his bloody prow from his stern. He can paint a proper ship.'

'There's also beauty in things that aren't familiar or pretty. Art recognises even strange subjects for their emotional power.'

Byrd grunted and dug into his pocket for a small leather purse. He undid it carefully and three pearls rolled onto the table. So they couldn't roll away he fenced in two of the pearls with cutlery. The third and biggest pearl he held up in his fingers.

'This is what beauty is,' he declared. 'A pearl. This pearl is beautiful. Everybody can see that.'

'Yes, it's beautiful in itself. And a very interesting creation. A mollusc dealing with an irritating grain of sand. But a pearl withholds important emotion until it's given to someone as a token of love.'

Byrd shook his head. 'The beauty of this pearl is understood by the world. It's how I've come by this schooner and another twenty-two boats besides. The world's belief in its beauty is why I can provide you free passage to indulge your art.'

'I'm grateful to pearls and to you. But to paint a pearl doesn't interest me. Nor is a painting of a pretty pearl worth a second look.'

'Is a painting of a malformed deckhand worth a second look?'

Nash took a deep breath. 'It's interesting to an artist to try to portray character in an unconventional subject. Baptiste's face is more confronting than, say, Lady Robinson's. It arouses stronger feelings.'

'I've no doubt of that!'

'I've painted people more marred and downtrodden than Baptiste, pictures full of meaning and passion. Paintings of the slave trade in the Americas, for example. Of whippings. Of African men dragging carts and being flogged like mules. A devastating lack of humanity and, I'd argue, powerful art.'

The captain returned the three pearls to his wallet, poured himself another whisky, took a long sip and gazed out to sea as if calming himself with the simultaneous sight of the sinking sun and the rising moon.

'A bloody far cry from beauty, those people,' he said.

*

Next morning Nash was sitting on deck sketching as the *Eileen* began provisioning those luggers working the pearling grounds around the Aru Islands. On these shallower beds, about five fathoms deep, some of the boats used Aboriginal divers. Today, five or six of them were preparing to dive from each lugger's dinghy.

In order to get nearer to the divers, Nash joined the impassive Malay diver in charge of one of the dinghies. As the man sculled against the tide to keep his boat stationary over the pearl beds, Nash sat near him at the stern, drawing the naked black divers. He tried to capture their synchronised submersions, the wildly rocking boat, as all the men descended together with ear-splitting yells.

The Malay sculler said the reason they dived in simultaneously was in order to cover the seabed methodically. But more probably because of their optimistic belief in the safety of numbers against sharks.

Abruptly, the divers kicked down and were swallowed by the ocean. With his pocket watch, Nash timed their stints underwater. Most of the men held their breath for about four minutes each submersion and one barrel-chested older fellow managed four-and-a-half minutes.

On rising to the surface, each diver swam to the boat, threw his catch of oysters over the gunwale and climbed aboard, nose streaming and chest heaving, to rest for a few minutes. Occasionally a diver brought up two or three oysters from a single dive, but four oysters in a dozen descents was more likely.

Back aboard the *Eileen* that afternoon, Nash was on deck perfecting his sketches of the bare-skin divers when Cribb came up and squatted beside him. He was smiling in an odd, confiding way.

'May I see your drawings, Nash? I've always been curious about the art world and its subject matter.' He gave a snort of apparent amusement. 'As a working man, I've also wondered what "work" is to an artist.'

With some hesitation, Nash passed them over. 'This is work, Mr Cribb. I spend many hours a day doing it, and support myself by selling it. But it isn't work if you think work means drudgery. It's not a chore. More a serious absorption. A contented concentration of mind and the skills I've learned.'

Without comment except for an occasional raised eyebrow, the mate examined the sketches in detail before handing them back. 'Very frank and true to life. Quite a skill indeed, to draw nudity. You didn't leave anything out.'

Then Cribb gazed out to sea and sighed deeply, as if choosing his words. 'I'm glad drawing those men makes you contented, Nash. But let me ask you something. Are you a married man?'

'Not as yet.'

'The captain and I were wondering. A girl in every port, eh, for you vagabond artists?'

'You're confusing artists with sailors, Mr Cribb.'

'The bohemian life doesn't lend itself to marriage, I imagine.'

'You can tell the captain I'm still a bachelor, Mr Cribb.'

'I think he understands that, Nash.'

*

That evening during dinner the captain and mate seemed preoccupied. They were huddled together in earnest conversation, murmuring and drinking whisky at one end of the table. Their distant demeanour towards him, and their frowns and occasional snorts of laughter, made Nash feel like an ignored fellow passenger in a London train carriage.

Eventually he shifted his seat, apologised for disturbing their conversation and introduced the subject of going ashore. 'All the sketching on a rolling deck has been useful and I've got something to show for it, but I need a steadier hand for painting. My aim is still to explore and paint a suitable island.'

The seamen looked at each other. 'Yes, *Hitherto unseen* by artists. I was just thinking the same thing,' Byrd said. 'We're nearing a pearling ground just off Veni Island. That island might nicely suit your purposes.' The mate nodded in agreement.

'Three days ashore would be welcome,' said Nash.

'We use Veni as a storm haven,' said the captain. 'There's a hut there and food supplies in case of cyclone emergencies. And a freshwater spring. It's the dry season now, the weather is clear and you should be comfortable enough.'

Next afternoon, an unseasonably warm and balmy day even for the Arafura Sea, the *Eileen* moored half a mile off Veni Island, and once the tide had turned and the reef instantly became a sweeping expanse of darting dorsal fins and stingray wings, Baptiste was instructed to row Nash, his painting materials and his dog ashore.

*

Following the old flipper prints and sand scrapes of nesting turtles, and the surging enthusiasm of Widdle – overexcited to be on dry land again – Nash climbed to the top of a steep dune and watched Baptiste's dinghy become a smaller and smaller speck on the ocean as it headed back to the *Eileen.*

From this vantage point he had a view of the whole island. It was more or less round, hardly three miles long and wide. Thick vegetation surrounded a swampy lake in its centre. Muddy inlets on the leeward side were choked by mangroves. The rest of its coastline was a flat tidal platform of rock rising to jagged limestone teeth and black volcanic cliffs.

A pair of sea eagles nested in the cliffs' serrations, and when Widdle raced around in boisterous circles, yapping and snuffling in the sand, the birds observed this nonsense for a few minutes before nonchalantly taking to the sky.

A hundred yards inland from the cliff tops, at the edge of a vine thicket and leaning away at an angle of about eighty degrees from the path of old monsoons, stood a small wooden hut, bleached to bone by the weather. It was locked.

Nash had brought some biscuits and salt meat with him, enough food for one day, two at a stretch, but not three. And hardly enough to share with Widdle. Captain Byrd had insisted the hut would provide food and shelter. The door, the most solid part of the ramshackle structure – really more a shed than a hut – wouldn't budge.

The sun was setting and the wind from the sea was picking up. Nash found a weathered and lichened plank on the hut's windward side and pulled it loose. But Widdle brushed past and beat him inside, leaping crazily at the squealing rats nesting there.

As for stores, although their labels had been gnawed off, there were six cans of food and four bottles of vinegar left unscathed. The rest of the supplies – dried peas and beans, sacks of flour and sugar and tea – had long since deteriorated, been eaten by rats or befouled.

A plank bench held a kerosene lamp, a tomahawk, a kitchen knife, a spoon, a tin dish and cup, a blackened pot, a can opener, a rusty bucket and three tins of matches, all sprinkled with rat droppings. As darkness fell, Nash lit the lamp and ate the biscuits he'd brought from the schooner. Widdle sniffed and nibbled curiously at a nest of pink newborn rats but lacked the resourcefulness to eat them.

The flickering lamplight wasn't strong enough for Nash to work. Nor did he want to. There was nothing to read. He and the dog lay on hessian sacks that stank of rat urine. The loose boards of the shed rattled in the wind and allowed entry to mosquitoes.

All night, small nocturnal mammals rustling and scratching outside the hut kept Widdle whimpering and twitching, dashing and growling.

*

Up early next morning, exhausted, thirsty and covered in mosquito bites, Nash observed the *Eileen* still anchored out to sea. Halfway to the horizon, the schooner looked as serene, clean-lined and simple as a child's drawing. Two luggers were moored nearby and he imagined that Byrd's helmeted divers were already working the pearl beds below the boats.

The tide was out and the island's shore ledge remained in slippery shadow. It was decorated with intricate artworks – the trails of slowly creeping shellfish and sea snails, creatures of ornate designs themselves, and many elaborate seaweeds and algae formations. Undersea lookalikes of necklaces and babies' brains and sausages and grapes and lettuces and tangled locks of mermaids' hair. Dotted across the tidal shelf were rock pools of many sizes and depths, most containing fat black sea-slugs as shiny as dancing shoes, and one or two with scalefish stranded by the tide.

Nash heard a sudden clattering like cutlery and saw the seaward cliff face swarming with red and green crabs, emerging from fissures and caves and spidering up and down the walls. Like uniformed guards they advanced aggressively, rattled their weapons in a show of forewarning, patrolled back and forth, clattered their claws some more, paused to rethink the situation, and scuttled back to safety.

Nature's vivid colours and skittish activity lifted his spirits, but even this early in the day the heat was becoming fierce and dehydrating. In the hut he opened a mystery food can for breakfast and ate what was revealed to be peaches. Sharing the syrup with the dog, he thought, *So, what are my priorities on a tropical island? First, water. Then, in order to profitably use my limited time here, work.*

He carried the bucket down to the lush patch of rainforest in the mid-distance that signalled the site of the freshwater spring. And shortly he and Widdle were soaking themselves and drinking from a spring that rose bubbling from within a swamp. The water was cloudy and had mosquito larvae and leeches. They drank anyway.

A full water bucket carried a mile back uphill was a different proposition to an empty bucket toted downhill. Choosing an easier indirect route back to the hut, he passed the coastal inlets where mud crabs the size of dinner plates sidled confidently behind portcullises of mangrove roots. Just in time he also noticed the nearest mud bank contained a large basking crocodile. Widdle instantly began barking. Gripping the dog's collar, and despite the bucket's weight, Nash hurried to higher ground and the hut.

By now the *Eileen* and the two luggers had sailed. All the way to the horizon the ocean was empty and still. For the first time since he'd left Broome there were no sounds to be heard beyond his own laboured breathing. No waves broke on the shore ledge and there was no trace of human activity beyond his own meagre efforts. No seabirds called. No fins broke the surface. What was strangest of all was to see no boats on the sea.

This arduous labour of water-gathering was only for two more days, Nash told himself next day, as he lugged the bucket back to the spring. He'd brought his sketch book this time, and sat by the swamp all morning drawing the bubbling spring and the eucalypt rainforest around it and wading birds and the purple dragonflies darting over the water for mosquito larvae and a pair of red goshawks watching him from a stringybark.

This was where the island's creatures lived. Their oasis. Widdle tore about, harassing a family of finches and some lorikeets rustling in the swamp reeds. When a long-beaked heron faced him down, Widdle backed off. And Nash drew all this, too.

*

By noon on his third day on the island, he'd painted two small seascapes from various cliff-top vantage points, made about twenty satisfactory sketches for later finishing, including – from a safe distance uphill, with Widdle tethered to a tree – two drawings of the mangrove forest and mudflats, and man and dog had finished all the canned food.

As he opened the last can – some sort of anonymous and gelatinous pale meat – he was struck momentarily with the reckless finality of this action, but then, *What does it matter?* He'd be back aboard the schooner by tonight.

In an amused mood he spent half an hour sketching the hut in all its decrepit, weather-beaten glory (titling it *Farewell to the Official Residence, Veni Island, Arafura Sea, 1899*) and then took his paintbox to the cliff top to await the *Eileen.*

His thinking was that he'd attempt a sort of island triptych. First panel: the bright midday appearance of a schooner over the horizon; next panel: mid-afternoon, the schooner is anchored midway and a dinghy rows towards the island; finally: the dinghy rows back to the schooner with its passengers – man and dog – against a brilliant sunset. Call it *Arafura Visitors.*

But this artistic tableau did not play out in real time. Of course timetables were capricious at sea. When the ocean was still empty on the fourth morning, his thought was that the *Eileen* had been slowed down by weather. *But the weather is fine.* Then an accident had delayed it. *Of course, that was it.* Pearling was a perilous tropical endeavour. Forget polite city schedules. At sea, disaster always threatened.

Be patient. It'll be here soon.

Strange how much further away the horizon seemed when you awaited an overdue boat. How much vaster the ocean and overbearing the sky. How stark the sudden change from disappointment to despair.

How much emptier the larder now, too. And how much hungrier the artist-exile. Though Widdle had changed his mind about eating rats and now also hunted successfully at night for marsupials, Nash had nothing to eat. It began to rain, a small mercy on this sleepless night. A tentative drizzle at first then a three-hour downpour, and at least Nash was sensible enough to put out the bucket.

*

For two days he sat on the cliff staring at the sea or lying mournfully on the rat-fouled sacks, eating small, easily collected shrimplike creatures he had no name for and that made him sick. But the dog whined so irritatingly at his helplessness that the next day he began to face the reality of his situation.

With the bucket baited with rat guts he learned to catch crabs and prawns in the rock pools overnight and some mornings he managed to scoop up a stranded fish or octopus from a tidal pool.

He chopped up the octopus with the tomahawk. Not a swimmer, he plucked up courage to jump into the shallows at low tide, duck underwater, hold his breath and pluck crayfish from the reef. With his palette knife he prised small oysters off the rocks. He survived on one daily meal of sea life that he cooked on a rock fireplace. And in nine days he'd used all the matches and kerosene.

For another day he struggled to keep down raw crabs and octopus before he remembered the artist's magnifier in his paintbox and thereafter ate his daily meal at noon when the sun allowed him to concentrate the rays and make a cooking fire. And a smoky signal fire of dry kelp on the cliff top every afternoon.

Six months passed on Veni Island. In summer, high winds and heavy rain lashed the island but at least during the Wet there was no need for the daily trip to the spring. In the sea he washed away the smell of rat piss from his bedding of sacks, but rain poured inside the hut and now it smelled of mould.

He was very thin. He had bleeding gums, leg sores and flaky skin. He thought this might be scurvy. If so, vinegar's reputation as a preventative proved wrong. He thought it strange at his young age to be in such a situation that the smell and clamminess of his own deteriorating body embarrassed him.

Now his days were strictly scheduled and based entirely around food, water and the sunset. Every dawn he clambered down to the tidal ledge to see what sustenance the night tide and stormy seas had entrapped. These mornings the catch was mostly inedible and venomous: chiefly washed-up sea snakes and jellyfish. The beauty of the sea snakes eluded him now. On the rare days of no rain he spent the morning fetching water from the spring and encouraging Widdle, only occasionally successfully, to catch swamp birds.

His ongoing hunger for the big mangrove crabs on the mud banks was frustrated by the constant presence there of the salt-water crocodile. Even when he couldn't see it he suspected it was lurking or submerged in the mangroves. Thankfully, the abundant dugongs and turtles of the Arafura Sea must have been satisfying its appetite.

If only a turtle or dugong would wash up on my tidal ledge, he said to himself. *I could kill it with the tomahawk.* In truth he doubted it.

It was wonderful Widdle who led him to the boobies roosting on high ground beyond the spring. Hundreds of the seabirds clustered on a wide rocky outcrop to nest together that summer, and even in his sickly condition it wasn't difficult to wade into the rookery and collect chicks and eggs, and one blow of the tomahawk easily dispatched an adult booby. The boobies' fat was good for frying; their flesh was delicate and filling, but though a change from fish, it was only a slight difference. Boobies tasted of fish.

For several weeks the boobies nested there and he ate wonderfully. Then one morning he arrived at the rookery to see them all take off together, all returning to the ocean to stock up again and feed hungrily, all gliding close to the ocean surface with languid wing beats, all skimming the waves and taking flying fish on the wing.

Despite the torrid heat at midday, the fire-lighting and cooking process now took him several hours in the humid swirling winds of summer and was impossible on wet or overcast days.

Late afternoon was both his best and worst time. Regardless of how weak he felt, he was always on the cliff top for what had become his only painting session of the day. Waiting for the sunset and trying to get the seascape right. Futilely trying to light a signal fire of kelp on the cliff top with his magnifying glass. Watching for the *Eileen* of course. Or any vessel at all.

Then one morning the heavy monsoon clouds lifted momentarily and he needed to visit the spring again for water. As he bent to dip the bucket into the flow, Widdle's barking suddenly had a shriller, more urgent note than the bluff tone the dog used for herons and lorikeets. They left in such a flurry that he spilled the water. The crocodile had moved residence to the swamp.

*

Back on the cliff top that afternoon he somehow convinced himself that thirst and the constant taste of blood in his mouth were not the problem. His physical condition, his shakes and loss of balance weren't the problem either. Food wasn't the problem. Anyway it hurt to chew with fewer teeth. He wasn't even too hungry any more.

The colour of the sea was still the problem. To be right, it depended on indigo. The amount of feeling he had for the potential of this painting was intensified by the constant lack of indigo. The whole predicament of his exile had narrowed down to the absence of indigo. An absence even more pressing with the extraordinary vividness of the summer sunsets, like Michelangelo's visions of heaven.

Sunsets in the Arafura Sea need a lot of indigo, he said to himself, aloud, yet again. He addressed himself aloud nowadays to ensure he heard and paid attention. Even then he sometimes didn't take sufficient notice and he had to raise his voice to a shout, especially when the cyclonic winds shrieked across the island and tore the frail boards from his hut and the pelting rain sent him and Widdle crouching under sacks in a corner.

When this habit of addressing himself had begun, the dog at first presumed he was talking to him. Now Widdle ignored every command except the whistle. The dog's every waking moment was a search for food. By no means had Widdle rid himself of the hunger problem.

Approaching sunset, Widdle was hungrily prowling the shore ledge below the cliff on rickety legs, scrabbling after tiny translucent ghost crabs, urgently and optimistically nosing stones and shells and ocean flotsam. When he eventually obeyed Nash's faint whistle and laboured up the dune to the cliff top, Nash noticed the dog's muzzle was stained a darkish blue.

'What have you bitten?' Nash said. Widdle still had a crushed shellfish in his mouth. One of thousands of the ovoid black molluscs that lay washed up in piles on the tidal ledge after the storms.

Nash took the dog's slobbery chin in his hands and removed the broken shell from his jaws. When Widdle licked him, he spread more blue dye on his wrist. More blue liquid, copious liquid, squirted from the shellfish meat.

On the cliff top facing the ritual of the sunset in the Arafura Sea, Nash declared to himself that if any painter were to give this shellfish dye a colour, they would have to say, as he did now, shouting into the wind, that it was indigo. True indigo.

Acknowledgements

For its support for this collection of stories I'm grateful to the Literature Program of the Australia Council. And to Nikki Christer, Rachel Scully, Fiona Inglis, Ben Ball, Alex Ross, Katie Purvis, Elizabeth Rich, and Brent Johnson.

'Dr Pacific' was first published in *Sex & Death* (Faber & Faber, London and New York), and *PLUK* magazine (Amsterdam); 'Paleface and the Panther' in *Brothers & Sisters* (Allen & Unwin, Sydney) and *The Best Australian Stories 2010* (Black Inc., Melbourne); 'Lavender Bay Noir' as 'The Razor' in *Sydney Noir* (Akashic Books, New York); 'A View of Mt Warning' in *Ten Stories You Must Read: Books Alive Guide* (Australia Council, Sydney); and 'Black Lake and Sugarcane Road' in the *Kenyon Review* (Ohio).

Some characters in 'Black Lake and Sugarcane Road' have appeared in previous fiction, while earlier versions of 'Varadero' were published in *Westerly* and *Gourmet Traveller.*

The story 'Imaginary Islands' continues, a generation later, with characters from the Lang family in *The Bodysurfers.*

Perhaps I should also acknowledge a favourite song, 'Beyond the Sea' (Jack Lawrence, 1945), a cover of 'La Mer', words and lyrics by Charles Trenet the same year, and recorded ever since by everyone from Bobby Darin to Robbie Williams.